Amber was stunning—next to her, all the other women seemed plain.

And that unsettled him. He'd been here before. Lost his heart and his head to a gorgeous media darling. Married her within a month. And he'd really repented at leisure.

Not that he had any intention of getting involved with Amber. He wasn't looking for a relationship. Not right now, when his life was such a mess. He needed to focus on getting his career back on track. On finding a cure for his loss of smell. He couldn't afford to let his libido get in the way.

Amber smiled at him. "Excuse me, Guy. I enjoyed our chat. Catch you later."

And then she was gone.

Funny how his little corner of the terrace had suddenly lost its brightness. Guy shook himself. She wasn't his type. And he'd be crazy to let himself think otherwise.

KATE HARDY lives in Norwich, in the east of England, with her husband, two young children and too many books to count! When she's not busy writing romance or researching local history, she helps out at her children's schools—she's a school governor and chair of the Parent and Teacher Association. She also loves cooking— see if you can spot the recipes sneaked into her books! (They're also on her website, along with extracts and stories behind the books.)

Writing for Harlequin Books has been a dream come true for Kate—something she'd wanted to do ever since she was twelve. She's been writing Harlequin® Medical Romances for more than five years now, and also writes for the Harlequin Presents line. She says it's the best of both worlds, because she gets to learn lots of new things when she's researching the background to a book—add a touch of passion, drama and danger, a new gorgeous hero every time, and it's the perfect job!

Kate's always delighted to hear from readers, so do drop in to her website at www.katehardy.com.

CHAMPAGNE WITH A CELEBRITY

KATE HARDY

~ ONE NIGHT AT A WEDDING ~

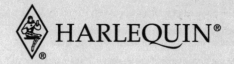

HARLEQUIN®

TORONTO • NEW YORK • LONDON
AMSTERDAM • PARIS • SYDNEY • HAMBURG
STOCKHOLM • ATHENS • TOKYO • MILAN • MADRID
PRAGUE • WARSAW • BUDAPEST • AUCKLAND

Recycling programs
for this product may
not exist in your area.

ISBN-13: 978-0-373-52799-1

CHAMPAGNE WITH A CELEBRITY

First North American Publication 2011

Copyright © 2010 by Pamela Brooks

www.eHarlequin.com

Printed in U.S.A.

CHAMPAGNE WITH
A CELEBRITY

CHAPTER ONE

WE'LL have to wait and see. The phrase that Guy had come to hate most in the entire world. How the hell could he be patient about this, when it could turn his entire world upside down?

But this was the second specialist to say it. His third medical opinion in as many months. And while 'we'll have to wait and see if your sense of smell returns' might be perfectly acceptable advice for most people, it absolutely wasn't fine for a parfumier. Guy couldn't do his job properly without his sense of smell.

He'd been covering it up for three months now. It was only a matter of time before someone found out. And then things would get seriously difficult; as it was, his business partner wanted to accept a huge conglomerate's offer to buy out the perfume house. Guy had resisted, so far—he wanted to keep them focused on what their customers wanted, and continue to support local suppliers—but this would give Philippe the ammunition he needed to force the sale. How could GL Parfums possibly continue as it was, when its head of research and development had lost his 'nose'?

Hell, hell, hell.

He'd been banking on this last specialist being able to help him. On being able to offer him something more than just waiting to see if it cleared up by itself, because the only possible reason for it was damage caused by the virus. He'd sat perfectly still and gone through the truly nasty procedure of having a camera on a tube fed up his nose and into his sinuses. He'd taken vitamin supplements. He'd spent hours online, scouring every possibility, reading the forums of every support group. And still he was being told, 'We'll have to wait and see.'

Worse, the specialist had added that it could take up to three years for his sense of smell to come back, and even then it might not come back fully.

Three *years*?

The last three months had been bad enough.

The prospect of spending three years like this was torture.

Besides, he couldn't wait for three years. The perfume house couldn't afford to stand still—if they didn't develop new fragrances or extend their current lines, they'd have no chance of competing in the market. And then it would go under and everyone would lose their jobs. His staff had supported him and believed in his dreams so much that they'd even taken a pay cut, in the early days, to keep the perfume house going. How could he let them down?

Unless he hired someone to be his 'nose' at the perfume house in his stead…and then his own role would have to change. He'd have to shoulder a lot more of the admin and the marketing—the things he'd always been relaxed about delegating, because he'd been happiest in his lab developing new fragrances. Hiring another parfumier would mean that he could keep the perfume house going; but it also meant that the perfume house would stop being his dream. It'd just be a job. He'd be living half a life, unable to do what he loved most: the thing that got him up in the mornings and made him glad to be alive.

He knew it was selfish of him—and unfair—but he really didn't think he could bear that.

Thank God he'd finalised the formula for the new perfume before his sense of smell had gone. That would buy him a few more months. And then he'd just have to hope to hell that whatever the problem was with his nose could be fixed. That he could find a specialist who could help him.

And somehow he had to drag himself back from the brink so he could be smiling, urbane, sweet-natured Guy Lefèvre, best man at his brother's wedding. He wasn't going to drop the vaguest hint that his life was turning into a nightmare: no way was he going to ruin Xav and Allie's happiness with his own misery.

'Smile,' he told himself harshly, 'and look as if you mean it.' And he was supposed to be out here cutting roses for the table arrangements, not making clandestine calls on his mobile phone to an ENT specialist and brooding in his garden. Better get on with it, before someone came to find out what was taking him so long.

'Sheryl, it's gorgeous. It's just like what I expected a French château to be like. Did you get the photo I sent you?' Amber asked.

'Yes. All tall windows and old stone. Very glam.'

'It's a bit shabby inside,' Amber admitted, 'but a little bit of work could fix that. Change the faded drapes for voile and light damask, paint the walls white with just a hint of rose, and get someone to polish the parquet and the panelling. And there's this amazing chandelier in the hallway. Needs cleaning, mind, but it's a stunner.'

Sheryl laughed. 'Don't tell me you're going to persuade Allie to lend you the place for a party?'

'I'm tempted,' Amber admitted. 'How much would

people pay for a weekend house party in France, do you think? Or maybe a Marie Antoinette–themed dinner?'

'I don't believe you. You're meant to be having fun at a wedding, and you're spotting locations for a possible charity ball.'

'Well, yeah. It's gorgeous, Sher. The kitchen's to die for. It's enormous. There's this old terracotta floor, cream-painted cabinets—and they're obviously handmade—gleaming copper pans and a scrubbed wooden table.' The kind of kitchen she would love to have, herself.

'Just as well the paps can't hear you,' Sheryl teased. 'If only they knew that Bambi Wynne the party girl likes being all domesticated.'

'Just as well you won't tell them, then,' Amber retorted, knowing that her best friend was completely trustworthy and would never betray her to the media. She pushed away the thought that she'd actually quite like to be domesticated, pottering round at home with a family to settle down with. Being the centre of someone's world.

How ridiculous.

She had a fabulous life—one that most people would envy. A nice flat in a fashionable part of London; good friends to meet for lunch and go shopping with; invitations to celebrity parties and cinema premières. Her time was her own, and if she fancied shopping in Milan, Paris or New York she could just hop on a plane without having to worry. She was on decent terms with all her family, so why on earth would she have this hankering to be tied down?

She shook herself. 'And the rose garden here. I've never seen so many in one place before. You know that corner of the handmade soap shop we like in Covent Garden? Walking through here's even better than that. Like drinking roses every time you breathe in.' On impulse, she wandered over to one choice bloom and picked it. She sniffed deeply and sighed. 'This has to be the most beautiful scent in the world.'

Guy rounded the corner and stared in disbelief.

Véra?

Common sense kicked in. No, of course Xav wouldn't have invited his ex to the wedding. Even if Allie knew her through work, he very much doubted that she and Véra would be friends. Allie wasn't in the least bit princessy, whereas his ex-wife had turned out to be a demanding, selfish diva. More fool him for letting his heart rule his head and not letting himself see what she was really like before he'd married her.

Then the woman turned, and Guy realised that he'd actually been holding his breath.

It wasn't Véra.

Though this woman was physically very like his ex: tall and slender, with legs that went on for ever. She wore her hair the same way, in long, dark spiral curls; even though Guy knew better than to act on the impulse, his fingers tingled with the urge to find out if they felt as silky as they looked. And he'd just bet that under those dark glasses she'd have huge blue eyes, enhanced by coloured contact lenses and super-volumising mascara to make them even more striking.

She was obviously one of the wedding guests. One of Allie's friends, he guessed, because she looked the media type—she was beautifully groomed, even in jeans and a T-shirt. And she was chatting happily on her mobile phone as she strolled through the roses, gesturing with her free hand. She looked absolutely carefree.

And then, to his shock, she stooped and snapped off one of the roses.

Oh, now this really *wasn't* on. He didn't mind people wandering in his garden, but he *did* mind them interfering with his roses. What would she do next—toss it to the ground and tread on it, now it had served her whim?

He strode over to her. 'Excuse me.'

She looked up. 'Oh. Got to go, call you later,' she said swiftly into her phone, and ended the call before giving him the most dazzling smile. 'Sorry about that. Was there something you wanted?'

He gestured to the rose in her hand. 'Don't you think you should ask first?'

She frowned. 'It's beautiful, and flowers are for sharing. I didn't think Allie and Xav would mind if I picked a single rose for my room.'

'It's not their garden,' he pointed out. 'It's mine.'

'Oh.' Colour bloomed in her cheeks, making her skin look as pink and as soft as the rose in her hand. 'Well, in that case, I apologise.' She gave a disarming shrug and another of those sweet, sweet smiles. 'I guess it's a tad late to ask permission now.'

She pushed her sunglasses up over her forehead to the crown of her head, and Guy felt his body tighten. She didn't have blue eyes. They were a deep, deep brown, and absolutely enormous. And, from his time with Véra, he could tell that she wasn't wearing much make-up at all: not even mascara to define those amazing eyes. Just the barest sheen of lipstick. Then again, she didn't actually need make-up. She had to be the most beautiful woman he'd ever met, including the days when Guy had been married to a supermodel and had mixed with some of the most gorgeous women in the world.

And no doubt she knew just how stunning she was, because she bent her head slightly to sniff the rose, looking up at him. The perfect coquettish pose—one that was very close to his ex's trademark.

'This really is the most amazing scent,' she said.

He knew that. Except he couldn't smell it any more. Only something like the ghost of a scent—so it was more likely that he was simply remembering what they smelled like instead of actually smelling them. And memory wasn't enough. 'Yes,' he said, through gritted teeth.

'I didn't think roses would still be blooming at the end of September.' She shrugged and smiled. 'Still, I guess this is the Med. Or near enough.'

He knew he ought to be polite. She was a guest in his home. It wasn't her fault that he couldn't smell, and it certainly wasn't her fault that she reminded him of Véra. But she'd pressed all his buttons; he was nearly crazy with the frustration of not being able to fix the two biggest problems in his life; and the strain of keeping it from those he loved most—because he knew they already had enough on their plate and didn't need the extra worry about him—wasn't doing a lot for his temper.

'If you don't know where we are, try looking at a map,' he suggested. 'And kindly don't damage any more of my roses.' He turned on his heel and walked off, without a backward glance. He needed to get out of here. Now. Allie's roses would just have to wait.

Amber stared at the man's retreating back.

Wow.

What had she done? Were these prize-winning roses and he was the gardener, or something? It would certainly explain why there were so many roses around here. Didn't posh gardeners have lots of different varieties though, and pride themselves on breeding different ones? Most of these roses seemed to be the same colour, cream at the centre shading to a deep blush-pink at the edges.

And what did he mean, it was his garden? Surely it belonged to the château and the vineyard? Or maybe he'd been the gardener here for years and felt that it was 'his' spiritually.

All that suppressed anger, over one little rose.

Crazy.

Though she felt a tiny bit guilty. He was right about one thing: she was a guest, and she should've resisted the impulse to pick a rose for her room. Or at least asked first.

Never mind. She'd ask Allie about her gorgeous sexy gardener—and if he ever smiled. Because, even though he'd been all brooding and simmering, she'd noticed how gorgeous he was. Sun-bleached fair hair, eyes the colour of a summer evening sky and a mouth that promised passion, all wrapped up with a seriously hot body.

She rolled her eyes. Picking a rose, without asking, was enough of a gaffe. Seducing her friend's gardener would definitely be off limits. Besides, after that embarrassing feature in *Celebrity Life* a month ago—detailing every single one of her boyfriends over the past year, how long they'd lasted and how they'd dumped her—she'd decided to steer clear of men for a while.

She headed back to her room, filled the glass in her bathroom with water and put the rose in it, then placed it on the table next to her bed.

This place was so gorgeous. OK, so the walls needed a lick of paint and the heavy gold damask curtains were faded and the rug was a bit threadbare, but the half-tester bed was like a fairy princess's. The whole place screamed 'shabby chic' and history. And her room had the most amazing view over the rose garden. It was the kind of room where you'd be quite happy to get up early in the morning, because you'd get to see the sun rising over the garden.

Lucky Allie, having all this at her disposal.

And definitely lucky her, having a friend who could invite her to stay somewhere so fabulous.

She wandered down to the kitchen; Allie was sitting at the kitchen table with someone else she recognised and hadn't seen for ages. 'Gina!' She gave the designer a huge hug, kissing both cheeks. 'When did you get here?'

'The taxi dropped me off ten minutes ago.'

She rolled her eyes. 'You should've texted me. I could've waited at the airport for you and given you a lift. Never mind.' She hugged her again. 'It's so lovely to see you.'

'The coffee's hot, if you want some,' Allie said with a smile.

'Yes, please.' She poured herself a mug from the cafetière and added a splash of milk. 'By the way, Allie, I'm sorry. I'm afraid I've just upset your gardener.'

'My gardener?' Allie looked surprised.

'He caught me picking one of the roses. He was a bit cross with me.'

Allie frowned. 'I don't have a gard—oh, wait. Was he tall, blond and gorgeous?'

'Tall and blond, yes.' Amber shrugged. 'Gorgeous…' Definitely. 'He might be, if he wasn't scowling.'

Allie blinked. 'Guy never scowls.'

'Who's Guy?' Amber asked.

'Xav's brother. It's his château.'

Oh. So it really *was* his garden. Amber bit her lip. 'In that case, I owe him an apology.'

'Sorry, it's my fault. I should've warned you that he's precious about his roses, so don't touch them.'

'He's a garden expert?'

'Parfumier,' Allie corrected. 'You've heard of GL

Parfums?' At Amber's nod, she said, 'That's him. Guy Lefèvre.'

'GL Parfums? They do that fantastic shower gel. The citrussy one,' Gina said. 'They were going on about it in *Celebrity Life*, the other week, about how it was the best pick-me-up ever.'

Amber groaned. 'Don't mention *them*.'

Gina hugged her. 'They gave you quite a mauling last month, didn't they?'

'Mmm, and how the hell did they find out that Raoul the Rat dumped me by text? I swear they must be tapping my mobile.' She deliberately kept her voice light, but that feature had hurt. And Raoul had hurt her badly. She'd thought he was different, that he might be The One—but he'd turned out to be yet another of the liars and losers she always seemed to date. Sometimes she thought it was as if she had a tattoo on her forehead that was invisible when she looked in the mirror, but was written in neon colours for everyone else. *Shallow and heartless? Take me, I'm yours!*

She shook herself. 'Let's talk about something nicer. So that's his fragrance, is it?'

Allie nodded. 'That was the first scent Guy made for the perfume house. Originally it was an aftershave, but then he extended the line. Actually, Gina, I know he wants to talk to you because he likes what you did for our labels. He said something about a new project.'

'Really? Oh, I'd love the chance to work with him,' Gina said, looking enthusiastic. 'His perfumes are brilliant and it'd be a fantastic opportunity for me to be involved in designing packaging or what have you for a new perfume.'

Xav strolled into the kitchen, wrapped his arms round his wife-to-be and kissed her. 'Have you seen Guy anywhere, *ma belle*?'

'No, though we were just talking about him being a genius with scent,' Allie said.

'Then he's probably sneaked off to his lab,' Xav said, and kissed her again. 'I'd better go and fish him out, because we have a hot date with a barbecue lined up.'

'That's a terrible pun,' Allie said, laughing. 'Hot date with a barbecue, indeed.' She glanced at her watch. 'We'd better get started on the salads, I guess.'

'Count me in for kitchen duties,' Amber said as Xav left the kitchen. 'Important things first: what are you doing for pudding?'

'Pudding?' Allie's eyes went wide. 'Oh, no. I forgot pudding. How could I do that?'

'Because you're getting married tomorrow and have a dozen more pressing things to think about?' Amber suggested.

Allie sighed. 'I'd better run down to the village and get something from Nicole's. She makes the best *tarte tatin* in the world.'

Amber couldn't resist the opportunity of getting her hands properly on this kitchen. 'I could make pudding,' she said. 'We had this amazing one at the ball last month.' She pulled up some of the photographs on her phone to show them.

'Oh, wow, that looks fantastic,' Gina said.

'And it tastes even better. Is there somewhere in the village that'd sell raspberries and passion fruit?'

'Nicole's farm shop,' Allie said.

'Righty—I'll go shopping. Allie, if you could chat up your scary brother-in-law and wheedle three roses out of him, I'll be right back.'

'Are you sure you don't mind?'

'Course not. Is there anything else you need?'

'No.'

But Amber could see in her face that Allie was having an attack of butterflies. If this Nicole made great pastries, hopefully she'd sell chocolate as well. Cake would do, at a pinch.

It didn't take long to buy the ingredients she needed. She drove back to the château, then put her hair into a ponytail, ready to start cooking. 'Oh—before I forget. Butterfly-taming material,' she said with a smile, handing over the chocolates.

'You're wonderful. And I got what you asked for.' Allie produced three roses.

'Fantastic. I'm going to play.' Amber carefully painted the petals with egg-white, dipped them in icing sugar and set them to dry while Gina and Allie were in charge of the salads. She cooked the meringue and prepared as much of the filling as she could. 'I need to assemble this at the very last minute, or it'll be soggy and disgusting,' she said, 'so I'll do it when people have nearly finished eating, OK?'

'More than OK,' Allie said, giving her a hug. 'I don't know why *Celebrity Life* keeps making you out to be an airhead. They really have no idea about who you really are.'

Amber knew exactly why they did it. She'd turned down a date with one of the journos and, even though she thought she'd been tactful in her refusal, he'd really taken a huff. As a result, the magazine's favourite sport seemed to be Amber-baiting. She tried her best to ignore the snide headlines—When will Bambi be a Wynne-r in love?—but it was starting to rankle. After that last nasty feature, she'd had to stop herself going to the office and punching him on the nose. Ignoring him was the best policy. She'd just have to grit her teeth; someone else would do something indiscreet, soon enough, to take the spotlight off her.

'Who cares about *Celebrity Life*?' she said lightly, and picked up a platter of bread to take out to the terrace.

Xav was already cooking things on the grill, and Guy was pouring wine for all the wedding guests who were staying overnight at the château.

He handed her a glass in silence.

Time to fix things, she thought. She was definitely in the wrong about the rose, and it wouldn't be fair for Allie and Xav to have needless tension at their wedding. 'Guy, may I have a word, please?' she asked.

He looked wary. 'Why?'

'I owe you an apology,' she said, 'for picking your flowers without asking. Especially as I didn't have the manners to introduce myself when we met. I know your name and that you're Xav's brother. I'm Amber Wynne. Nice to meet you.' She held out her hand to shake his.

For a moment, she thought he was going to refuse, but then he took her hand and shook it. The second his skin touched hers, desire jolted through her, shocking her with its intensity; judging by the surprise in his eyes, quickly masked, it was the same for him.

Interesting.

Except, she reminded herself, she was off men. Her love life was a disaster area, and she'd promised herself a break for the next six months.

'I owe you an apology, too, Amber,' he said, surprising her. 'You're a guest and I shouldn't have snapped at you. My only excuse is that you caught me at a bad time.'

'And your roses are important to you. I thought you were maybe the gardener,' Amber said, 'but I take it that you grow them for your perfume?'

Guy looked slightly taken aback, clearly realising that she'd talked to Allie about him. 'Well, yes.'

'May I?' She gestured to the chair next to him. At his

brief nod, she sat down. 'You have a beautiful garden,' she said, 'and a beautiful home.' And she really hoped he hadn't overheard her telling Sheryl that it needed a bit of work. 'Thank you so much for letting me stay here.'

He shrugged. 'You're a wedding guest—any friend of my sister-in-law-to-be is a friend of my family.'

Guy had been prepared to dislike Amber, because she reminded him so much of Véra, but there was an easy warmth about her; to his surprise, he found himself relaxing and chatting to her. And when she encouraged him to talk more about his roses, for one crazy moment he thought he could smell them. On her skin.

No. Of course not. The virus he'd caught three months ago had put paid to that. But, all the same, she intrigued him.

And attracted him. An attraction he wouldn't let himself act on—not while his life was in chaos and all his energy seemed to be used up in fighting the fear that the career he loved was over. Besides, she was only here for the wedding. It wasn't as if their paths were likely to cross again in the near future. There was no point in starting something he had no intention of continuing.

When Allie and Gina started to clear away, Amber stood up and started helping—something else Guy hadn't expected. Véra would have considered herself a guest and therefore someone to be waited on, not someone to help with the waiting.

As if she read the expression on his face, she said, 'I'm in charge of pudding. Back in a minute.' She smiled, and was gone.

And what a pudding. She came back holding a platter containing two soft meringue roulades, filled with what looked like some kind of cream-and-fruit mixture; the top was decorated with candied rose-petals and a drizzle of passion-fruit seeds, and she'd found some indoor sparklers somewhere and stuck those in, too, so her pudding could make a real entrance.

'So that's why Allie wanted three more roses,' he said when she brought him a slice neatly plated.

She looked awkward. 'Sorry, but they were so perfect for this—cream in the centre shading out to deep pink at the edges.'

'And candying them must've taken you a while.'

'It's the little details that make the difference,' she said simply.

'And you pay attention to them.' Again, he hadn't expected that. He'd pigeonholed her as a careless, thoughtless diva. How had she managed to wrong foot him so completely? He gestured to the pudding to cover his awkwardness. 'This looks good. Are you a chef?'

She shook her head. 'I like messing about in the kitchen. But being a chef would mean working crazy hours. Not my thing.'

'So what is your thing?' he asked, suddenly curious.

'I organise parties.'

He blinked. 'You organise parties?'

'It's how I met Allie. She came to one of my parties, a couple of years back, and we hit it off. We've become friends.'

'You're a party girl.' So he'd been right, at heart. She *was* a media darling—just like his ex-wife.

'Uh-huh.' She sighed. 'But don't believe everything you see in the press about me.'

'You're in the press a lot?' Although her face seemed familiar, he couldn't quite place her. He skimmed the business news, most of the time online because it was quicker; he certainly didn't read the gossip and celeb pages in the newspapers, and the only time he saw one of the celeb magazines was if the cuttings agency sent it over because it contained a piece about GL Parfums. One of the things that drove his business partner, Phillipe, crazy was Guy's insistence on low-key product launches—but Guy had already been burned by the media. Badly. And he wasn't giving them a chance to dig around in his life again.

'She's the darling of the celeb mags, our Bambi,' Gina said, coming over and draping her arms round Amber's neck.

'Bambi?' The question was out before he could stop it.

'Because of those big brown eyes and the legs up to her armpits. If she wasn't so nice,' Gina said cheerfully, 'we'd all hate her for looking this good. Everyone else has to work at it. Not her. She could be wearing a sack after having no sleep for a week, and she'd still manage to look glamorous and start setting a trend! Life just isn't fair.'

Amber laughed. 'Thank you for the compliment, Gina, but you have to credit my mother for giving me her genes. And if you'd let me get you out of your "I'm an artist so I must wear black" uniform and put you in some colour to show off that porcelain skin, beautiful auburn hair and those gorgeous eyes, there'd be a queue of men from here to Paris.'

'No chance. I'm an *artist*,' Gina retorted, returning the grin.

'Hopeless,' Amber said, rolling her eyes. 'Tell her, Guy. She's gorgeous.'

'She's gorgeous,' Guy said dutifully. Gina was pretty enough. But Amber was stunning: next to her, all the other women seemed plain.

And that unsettled him. He'd been here before. Lost his

heart and his head to a gorgeous media darling. Married her within a month. And he'd really repented at leisure.

Not that he had any intention of getting involved with Amber. Even if she didn't remind him of the biggest mistake of his life, he wasn't looking for a relationship. Not right now, when his life was such a mess. He needed to focus on getting his career back on track. On finding a cure for his loss of smell. He couldn't afford to let his libido get in the way.

'Come and help me with the coffee?' Gina asked.

'Sure.' Amber smiled at her. 'Excuse me, Guy. I enjoyed our chat. Catch you later.'

And then she was gone.

Funny how his little corner of the terrace had suddenly lost its brightness. Guy shook himself. She wasn't his type. And he'd be crazy to let himself think otherwise.

CHAPTER TWO

THE next morning, Amber was awake before the alarm on her mobile phone went off. She had a quick shower and washed her hair, then headed for the kitchen. Allie and Gina were already there, having breakfast; she joined them, then did their nails afterwards and then made them sit to dry their nails properly while she sorted out the washing up.

Next was make-up and hair; and she was intrigued by the differences between a French wedding and an English one. 'So you have two wedding ceremonies—the official one at the *Mairie*, where you wear a business suit, and then at the church, where you have the white dress?' she asked.

'That's right,' Allie confirmed.

'Two weddings. That's just *greedy*,' Amber said, laughing. She stood back to look at her handiwork. 'Oh, Allie— Xav's going to take one look at you and then be desperate to carry you off to his lair.'

'You look stunning,' Gina agreed. 'Radiant.'

Allie flapped a dismissive hand. 'Ah, that's what you're supposed to say to all brides.'

'But it's still true,' Amber said. She pushed back the tiny bit of wistfulness: ridiculous. Right at the moment, she didn't even want to date anyone, let alone get married and settle down.

When Amélie, the flower-girl, arrived, Amber sat on the floor with her and taught her a counting song to make her feel less shy and more at ease, then did her hair, too.

'I look like a princess!' the little girl exclaimed in French when Amber showed her in the mirror.

'You certainly do,' Amber said, giving her a hug. 'Absolutely beautiful. And now I'd better get ready myself. See you all in a bit!'

Guy stared as Amber walked out of the château. Yesterday, in jeans and a T-shirt, she'd been stunning enough. But, dressed up, she was unbelievably gorgeous. As elegant as Audrey Hepburn, in a gold silk dress with spaghetti straps and matching strappy sandals; and her hair was piled on top of her head, secured with pearl-headed pins.

He was glad that he'd offered to drive some of the wedding party to the *Mairie*. At least concentrating on the road would keep his thoughts off Amber. Her smile, warm and bright and yet with a hint of unexpected shyness, made heat coil low in his belly and desire creep all the way up his spine. Worse still, his fingers itched to take the pins out of her hair and tumble her curls over her shoulders. And then he had a thought that really stopped him in his tracks: the idea of her hair tumbled across his pillow.

Oh, hell—he really had to get a grip.

'*Bonjour*, Guy.' Her voice was soft, low-pitched, a little bit on the posh side. Sexy as hell. 'Allie says you're driving us. Thank you.'

'Pleasure,' he responded automatically. 'Grab a seat.'

When she climbed into the front seat next to him, he really wished he'd been more specific and told her to sit in the back. It took all his concentration to drive to the village, knowing that every time he changed gear his hand was only a few centimetres away from her thigh. Especially as the hemline of her dress had already ridden up above her knee to reveal smooth, touchable skin—and she didn't seem in the slightest bit aware of it! She was chatting happily about how this was the first time she'd ever been to a French wedding and she was dying to see the *croquembouche*, the wedding cake made from *choux* buns held together in a pyramid with caramel.

This woman had the power to drive him crazy. Which made her very, very dangerous.

The wedding service at the *Mairie* was short and sweet; while Allie and Xav changed, the rest of the wedding party had a glass of wine in the café in the square, a couple of doors down, while they waited. Amber opted for a coffee rather than wine, wanting to pace herself; although she was chatting with some of the other guests, something made her break off mid-conversation and turn round.

And then she realised why.

Guy had walked into the café, looking stunning in a tailcoat, sky-blue waistcoat and matching cravat. Formal dress really suited him, and Amber wasn't surprised that all the other women in the coffee shop were staring at him, too. Guy Lefèvre was the kind of man who attracted attention, even though he didn't seem to be aware of it. There was just something about him and, when his gaze meshed with hers for a moment, her heart gave an odd little flip.

Oh, this was bad. Even if she wasn't officially being celibate, she couldn't possibly fall for Guy Lefèvre. He might not be one of the rats she usually dated, but she knew it would never work between them; they were from completely different worlds.

Then Allegra and Xavier appeared at the door. Allegra's

wedding dress was simple and elegant, in pure white; she
wore a simple tiara in her hair, and carried an exquisite
bouquet of white roses. Gina, as chief bridesmaid, was
holding Amélie the flower-girl's hand; both wore similar
dresses to Allegra's, but in the same sky-blue as Xavier
and Guy's waistcoats, and the little girl's dress had a deep
blue velvet sash round it.

The whole wedding party walked to the tiny church on
the edge of the village, led by the bride and groom; white
ribbons were strewn between the hedgerows, blocking their
path, until Allegra and Xavier cut them. Clearly this was
some kind of French tradition; Amber made a mental note
to ask Allie about it later. The church was ancient and
pretty, built in pale stone; inside, it was full of light. At the
altar there were two red velvet chairs placed beneath a silk
canopy—clearly waiting for the bride and groom—and as
they walked in Allegra's mother played the violin, a sweet
and haunting piece of Bach.

Although the service was conducted entirely in French,
Amber could just about follow what was going on. As
Allegra and Xavier exchanged rings Amber thought wistfully how lucky Allegra was to have found her one true
love. She didn't think she'd ever find one herself.

And then she was cross with herself for letting herself
be maudlin. She loved weddings and parties. And, as Allie
had claimed that French weddings went on all night and
finished at breakfast, Amber had every intention of having
a good time.

When the bride and groom had been showered in dried
delphinium petals outside the church and had stepped over
the laurel leaves strewn on the path, the champagne reception began in the churchyard. The *vin d'honneur*, or the
toast to the bride and groom: Amber knew that the whole
village was invited to this part. And when Xavier poured

a glass of champagne at the base of one of the gravestones and Allegra did the same to what looked like a much newer grave without a headstone, Amber realised it was a way of including those who were no longer with them—obviously Allie's great-uncle, and someone who presumably had been very close to Xav.

Back at the château, a huge marquee had been set up on the lawn, with tables edging a dance-floor. Time for the champagne reception. But what she hadn't expected was the way the champagne was opened. Guy and Xavier were both wielding curved sabres. They held the bottles with the corks pointing away from them, slid the sabres towards the corks and the corks flew out of the bottles with a short burst of champagne.

Amber had never seen anything like it. It was even more impressive than watching someone do a cascade of champagne glasses. If she could persuade Guy to teach her how to do it, it would be so fantastic for next year's midsummer ball.

Her chance to ask him came when she found herself unexpectedly seated next to him for the formal meal.

'That thing you did with the champagne was very impressive,' she said.

He lifted one shoulder. 'The *sabrage*, you mean?'

'It's not something I've seen before,' she said. 'So I take it that it's a traditional French thing?'

'Yes. It's from Napoleonic times—the Hussars celebrated victory by sabring the top off a bottle of champagne while they were still riding their horses at full gallop.'

And she could just imagine Guy in a Hussar officer's uniform. He'd look stunning on horseback. Sexy as hell.

With difficulty, she dragged her mind back to what he'd said. 'That sounds like a recipe for disaster, with glass flying all over the place—doesn't some of the glass get in the champagne?'

'No. The pressure of the champagne takes everything out.'

'How can you be so sure?'

Was she going to question everything he said? Guy wondered. Or was she really interested? To test her, he gave her all the facts and figures. 'It's a matter of holding the bottle at the right angle and hitting the lip of the bottle in the right place—at the seam, where it's weakest. And it's not a sharp sword—it's a champagne sabre, modelled on the design of the Hussars' swords.'

'So, with training, anyone could do it?'

'With training, yes.' And suddenly he realised the hole he'd just dug himself. Surely she wasn't going to ask him to let her have a go?

She smiled. 'Any chance of you teaching me?'

'Why would you want to learn that?' he parried.

'I already told you, I organise parties. And that includes a midsummer ball to raise funds for cancer research. Opening champagne like that at the ball would be spectacular—even better than the cascade of champagne glasses we did this year.'

'Why cancer research?' he asked.

'Because my favourite grandmother had breast cancer.' For a moment, a shadow crossed her face, but then she smiled. 'She's in remission right now, but this is my way of doing something to help.'

'Partying.'

'If you organise parties well and people have a good time, they're prepared to pay a lot of money for the tickets, which means the charity makes more,' she said. 'Sure, I could've done a sponsored walk or sat in a tub of baked beans or what have you, but this is more fun. It's a win-win situation for everyone.' She grimaced. 'And that wasn't meant to be a pun on my name.'

That sounded personal, Guy thought. No doubt the press enjoyed making puns with her name.

'Actually, I might as well be bold,' she said. 'As well as the money I make from the ticket sales, I hold a tombola to raise funds—big things, like a make-over, or a balloon flight, or a spa day, or a portrait by a really good photographer. I've managed to get dinner with a heart-throb in there too, by getting Mum to chat up one of her friends.'

'Your mother being…?'

'Libby Wynne, the actress.'

Oh, so *that* was why she looked familiar. Now he knew, he could see the resemblance. Though if pressed he'd say that Amber was even more beautiful than her mother.

'So, as you're this genius parfumier,' she continued, 'could I put you down for making a personalised scent for someone?'

It was the worst thing she could possibly have asked him.

Four months ago, he would probably have smiled and said yes. Now, he had no idea if he'd actually be able to do it. 'It's not just something you do on a whim,' he said coolly.

She spread her hands. 'Obviously there's more to it than just mixing a couple of oils together.'

'A lot more.'

'If designing a scent is too much to ask, maybe I could ask you for a gift basket instead—a big one?'

He wasn't sure if her chutzpah amused him or terrified him. 'You're utterly shameless, aren't you?'

'If you don't ask, you don't get.' She shrugged. 'What's the problem? I can't expect people to read my mind.'

What's the problem? he thought. My problem is that I'm incredibly attracted to you and I really don't need this. Not right now. 'Whatever,' he drawled. 'Put me down for a basket—just tell Allie nearer the time and I'll sort something out. And I'd better circulate a bit. We have dancing between courses, with this being a French wedding.' And please don't suggest I start dancing with you, he begged inwardly.

She didn't—and then he discovered he was disappointed that she hadn't asked.

Crazy.

He needed his head examined.

Amber recognised the tune of the first dance—'Time After Time.' It seemed to be traditional in France, too, that the newlyweds should start the dancing, followed by the best man and the chief bridesmaid. And such a beautiful song, she thought wistfully, mentally singing the lyrics. Would she ever find someone who'd catch her when she fell, someone who'd wait for her and support her? Judging by her past relationships, probably not; she always managed to pick the complete opposite.

She took a sip of her champagne. Enough of the pity party. This was a wedding, and she was going to have fun. There were loads of people here she hadn't met yet, and a few people who looked shy and a bit left out. One thing she was good at was getting a party going—and that was exactly what she planned to do.

Guy knew exactly where Amber was, even when his back was to her, because he could hear laughter. She was clearly working the party. Asking for more donations for her charity ball? he wondered, and sneaked a look.

No, she was fetching drinks for his great-aunts and

charming his great-uncles, and there was an approving smile on all their faces as she chatted with them. He was beginning to see why she organised parties: she had excellent people skills and the gift of putting people at their ease.

Then she went up to Allie's parents. This would definitely be worth watching, he thought, no longer hiding the fact that he was looking at her. The Beauchamps were notoriously standoffish; they'd been the parents from hell for Allie, and if Amber asked them to come and do a guest number at her ball, for nothing, he knew they'd send her away with a flea in her ear. They might even use it as an excuse to flounce off and fly back to wherever they were next playing a concert.

And then he blinked. Was he seeing things? Emma Beauchamp was actually smiling. Either Amber had met her before—and, even though she was a friend of Allie's, he thought that unlikely—or her people skills were even better than he'd thought. If she could thaw Emma Beauchamp, she could charm anyone.

He couldn't take his eyes off Amber. Clearly deciding that she'd schmoozed enough, she started dancing. But not on her own. And not a sexy, siren-type call to all the men who also couldn't take their eyes off her, either. No, she'd got all the children together in a group, and she was teaching them a simple routine. The girls all seemed thrilled that one of the grown-ups was paying them so much attention, and the boys were all clearly bowled over by her smile and couldn't do enough to please her. And their parents were all watching her with an indulgent smile; as soon as she noticed, she beckoned them to come up and join in. Within ten minutes, all the people who hadn't been dancing were up on their feet, joining in. And when one little girl slipped over, Amber scooped her up, gave her a cuddle to dry her tears and had her smiling again within a minute.

Amber clearly didn't care about grubby finger-marks, despite the fact that her dress was obviously expensive. She was all about *fun*.

Unable to resist the pull any longer, Guy fetched a flute of champagne and took it over to her. 'You look hot,' he said.

She dimpled at him. 'Now, are you saying my face is bright red, Monsieur Lefèvre, or was that an offer to dance with me?'

'Uh, I meant you've been dancing for ages and probably needed a drink, not that you look…' His voice faded and he could feel his own face heating. Especially as the look in her eyes told him that she knew he was lying. The attraction was mutual. He could tell by the way her lips parted, inviting him to kiss her—and it looked like an unconscious reaction rather than a planned seduction. 'All right. Both,' he admitted.

Her grin broadened. 'Well, hey. I did wonder if my dress was a bit too short.'

Above the knee. Yeah. He'd noticed. But her words made him look again.

For a moment, his tongue felt glued to the roof of his mouth. Then he called her bluff. 'Nice knees, Mademoiselle Wynne.'

'Why, thank you, Monsieur Lefèvre. And for the drink.' She took the glass, and it felt like an electric shock going through him when her fingers briefly brushed against his. And he definitely couldn't take his eyes off her mouth as she sipped delicately at the rim.

She had a beautiful mouth.

Irresistible.

And at that second he knew that, at some point tonight,

he was going to kiss her. And he knew that she'd be kissing him right back.

The jazz band switched into a number Amber recognised. The tango from the old Al Pacino film she'd watched with her mother a few months ago and loved. Even though she knew it'd be much more sensible to sit this one out and not bait Guy any further, her mouth wasn't working in sync with her brain. 'Dare you.'

'Dare me?' His eyes were suddenly very, very dark.

Shut up, Amber, shut up *now*, she warned herself. But her mouth was on a roll. 'Or can't you tango?'

'Challenging me, Amber? Isn't that a bit risky?'

Say no. Back off. Sit down, her brain telegraphed urgently.

Her mouth was having none of it. It smiled. Taunted him. 'Bite me, Guy.'

With slow, deliberate movements, he took the glass from her hand and set it down on the table. Then he yanked her into his arms, so his mouth was next to her ear. 'Bite you, hmm?' he drawled, his voice low and incredibly sexy. 'I'm taking that as an offer, *mon ange.*'

Amber was very, very glad that he was holding her up. Because she could imagine his teeth grazing her skin as he explored her all over with his mouth, and the idea sent her weak at the knees. Not to mention sending her pulse rate into overdrive.

It looked as if she'd just unleashed a monster.

There was no going back, because then Guy began to dance with her.

She'd danced with professionals, but it had felt nothing like this. With them, it had been choreography and patience. This was something more elemental, leaving her aware of every beat of blood through her body. Her body was reacting to his closeness, growing more aroused every time he spun her back into his body and wrapped his arms round her midriff, holding her close to him, sliding one leg between hers and encouraging her to do the same to him.

What would've been choreography with anyone else felt like a prelude to sex with Guy. A thigh pressed between hers. Another press, making her wonder what it would feel like to have his bare skin against hers, his legs tangled with hers. A withdrawal, as if he'd pulled out of her body, ready to surge back in as deeply as he could. Her body pressed against his, hip to hip and belly to belly and breast to breast. The scent of his skin, overlaid with a light citrussy fragrance that made her want to taste him.

Nothing existed except Guy and the music. Every nerve-end was concentrated on him—on the way his body touched hers, teasing and enticing and promising all at the same time.

And then she felt the brush of his lips against the bare skin of her shoulder, a feather-light contact that made a pulse beat hard between her legs.

His eyes were dark, a stormy blue in the evening light. Did he feel this same deep throb of desire? Was he thinking about what it would be like to kiss each other properly, hot and wet and urgent?

Bite me, she'd said.

And how she wanted to feel his mouth on her body. Teasing her. Arousing her. Taking her right over the edge.

And then the music came to an abrupt end. Shockingly so.

'Bravo, Mademoiselle Wynne,' Guy whispered in her ear in the final hold.

Amber was even more shocked when people actually clapped them.

Oh, no. Don't say they'd been the only dancers on the floor?

But when she glanced round, the dance-floor was empty.

This was bad. He was going to think she was a total show-off. And although she opened her mouth to speak, to tell him she hadn't meant this to happen, the words just wouldn't come. She didn't have a clue what to say.

Celebrity Life would have a field day with her, because she was behaving just like the airhead they always made her out to be.

'I'm sorry,' she whispered finally.

He drew closer, stooped slightly so that his breath fanned her ear. 'I'm not. That was…enlightening.'

And she was in too deep. Way too deep. 'Could I, um, get a glass of water or something?' she asked.

He raised an eyebrow, as if calling her a coward. 'Sure.' He escorted her over to the bar area, and ordered them both a glass of iced water. 'So where did you learn to dance like that?'

'I had lessons when I was in my teens.'

'And?'

She sighed. 'All right. I've dated a couple of dancers. And, because I organise the balls, I've talked a few professionals into coming and giving a display before the general dancing starts. One of them taught me to tango.'

'Like that?'

She laughed wryly. 'Hardly.' She'd never danced quite like that with anyone before.

'Why not?'

Because the dancer hadn't turned her on, the way Guy Lefèvre did. There hadn't been the chemistry—on either side. 'Let's just say I would've needed a Y chromosome for it to work,' she said drily.

Guy raised an eyebrow. 'Nicely put.'

'Maybe. I'm sorry. My mouth runs away with me. Thank you for the water.'

'Pleasure.' But he didn't move away and start circulating, as she'd expected. He sat down with her.

This should be relaxing. It was the first time she'd sat down since the jazz trio started playing. But it felt as if she were sitting on hot coals. She couldn't stop fidgeting.

'What's the matter, Amber?' he asked softly.

'Nothing.'

'Liar.'

She took a deep breath. 'How many more times do I have to apologise to you?'

'You don't.' He sighed, set his glass down and took her hand, pulling her to her feet. 'Come on.'

'What—you want to dance again?'

'It's noisy in here.' In silence, he shepherded her away from the marquee and the dancing, to the peace of the rose garden.

This was bad, Amber thought. Very bad. Leaving a wedding party before the bride and groom was incredibly rude—unless things were different in France, which she somehow doubted. And if anyone had noticed, it meant she'd have a lot of explaining to do tomorrow.

'Dance with me here,' he said softly.

She could still hear the music from the jazz trio, but here it was muted. Soft and dreamy and incredibly lovely. And the air was filled with the scent of roses. How could she resist stepping into his arms?

One of Guy's hands was splayed across the bare skin between her shoulders. His touch made her skin tingle—and she wanted more. Much more. She found herself moving closer, wrapping her arms tightly round him. His cheek was pressed against hers, and Amber wasn't sure which of them moved, but then his lips were brushing the corner of her mouth. Like gossamer, but it lit a fire deep inside her.

She kissed him back, still keeping it light.

In return, his mouth turned coaxing, drawing a line of tiny, nibbling kisses all the way along her lower lip.

With a small sigh of pleasure, she opened her mouth to let him deepen the kiss. And it was like nothing else she'd ever experienced. Nobody she'd ever kissed before had made her feel literally weak at the knees, making her hold onto him for dear life. Every stroke of his tongue, every touch of his skin against hers, stoked the desire higher and higher. Wanting more, she couldn't help pressing against him, shifting her stance slightly so that he could slide one thigh between hers—just as he'd done when they'd danced the tango, except this time there was no audience. Just the two of them.

Then he pulled back. 'This probably isn't a good idea.'

'No, it isn't,' she agreed.

'Tell me to stop.' He hooked his thumb into the strap of her dress and bared her shoulder before nibbling his way along it.

'I can't.' She undid his cravat, then the top three buttons of his shirt, and pressed her mouth against his throat in a hot, wet, demanding kiss.

'Amber.' His voice was husky. 'Last warning. Tell me to stop.'

She undid his waistcoat, then finished undoing his shirt. 'Go,' she whispered.

In response, Guy scooped her up into his arms and carried her into the house.

CHAPTER THREE

GUY paused at the top of the stairs, set her on her feet, backed her against the wall and kissed her again. Thoroughly. By the time he broke the kiss, Amber's knees felt decidedly weak, and she was forced to cling to the front of his shirt to hold herself up.

His gaze was hot and intense as he touched the backs of his fingers against her cheek. '*Alors, mon ange,*' he said, his voice low and soft and incredibly sexy. 'In the rose garden, I gave you the chance to stop. This really *is* your last warning. If we don't stop now, I'm going to take you to my bed.'

'I'd rather that was a promise than a threat.'

'A promise of what?'

'Pleasure. For both of us. Just for tonight.' She took a deep breath. 'I'm a disaster area when it comes to relationships. But there's a spark between you and me, and the way you danced with me…I can't ignore that.'

'I'm not exactly good at relationships, myself,' Guy told her. 'And I'm not looking to get involved with anyone.'

'Right. So we both know where we stand.' She stood on tiptoe, and pressed her mouth lightly against his. Nibbled his lower lip.

He gave an exclamation of what sounded like mingled

need and frustration, and kissed her back, his mouth hot and sweet and demanding.

Then he took her hand and led her to the end of the corridor. Not to her room, she noticed: he took her to his.

It turned out to be similar to hers, with a huge old-fashioned half-tester bed covered in pure white bed-linen. The walls were painted teal, and the heavy damask curtains were a similar shade, lightened with cream voile; there were rugs scattered across the polished wooden floor, and a landscape painting hung on one wall.

No doubt in some of the rooms there would be portraits of his ancestors—men in eighteenth-century costume who looked exactly like Guy, with those same amazing blue eyes and that sun-kissed hair.

And who knew? Maybe one of them had danced with a woman at a wedding, and the attraction had been so strong that he'd carried her up the stairs to this very same bed...

'Are you still sure you want to do this?' Guy asked softly.

She trailed a forefinger down his chest. He really could've been a model for one of his own perfume ads. Muscular without being overdeveloped, his skin burnished to gold by the sun and beautiful enough to make any woman want to reach out and touch him. 'Absolutely. I had these pictures in my head when you danced the tango with me,' she admitted softly.

His gaze was scorching. 'I hope they're the same pictures that were in mine.'

She did, too. 'There's only one way to find out.'

His response was to kiss her hard.

And then he took the pins from her hair, one by one, and laid them on his dressing table. He combed through her hair with his fingers, and nodded in satisfaction as it fell past her shoulders. 'I like that. And your hair's so soft. So silky.' He wound a strand round his finger, then released it again. *'Ravissante.'*

When he spoke in his own language, it was incredibly sexy. She licked her lower lip, wanting him to kiss her again; but instead he took her clothes off, very, very slowly. So slowly that it made her ache with need and want to push his hands away so she could rip them off, then rip off his own clothes and guide him into her body.

But Guy was being thorough. Methodical. Paying attention to the little details. A tiny mole on her shoulder, the crease of skin on her elbow, the softness of her curves. Almost as if he were learning her shape with his mouth and his hands. He unzipped her dress with incredible slowness and patience—and then let it drop on the floor while he stroked her skin.

'I love this lacy stuff. It's gorgeous. Like you.' He traced the edge of her camisole top with the tip of his forefinger. 'But it has to go, Amber. I need you naked. And I really, really need to be inside you.'

Oh-h-h.

She wanted that, too. So desperately.

He slipped one spaghetti strap down over her shoulder and kissed her bare skin. She closed her eyes and tipped her head back in offering to him; he took the hint and kissed a line across her throat, pausing to tease the spot where her pulse beat crazily, then moved to the other shoulder, nuzzling her skin. His hands rested lightly on her waist, and the heat of his mouth against her skin was driving her mad. By the time he'd stripped her down to just her lacy knickers, she was quivering.

He looked gorgeous, with his shirt and waistcoat open and his cravat undone, but she needed to do more than just look. She needed to touch. To feel. To explore him, the same way he'd just explored her. Curve for curve, touch for touch.

'You're wearing too much,' she said shakily.

'I'm in your hands.'

The waistcoat went first, and then she pushed the soft cotton of his shirt off his shoulders, tracing the line of his collarbone as she did so. His skin felt glorious, soft and smooth, and there was just the right amount of chest hair to be sexy; she couldn't resist trailing her fingers across it.

'You have lovely hands,' he said, his eyes darkening. Giving her permission to go further.

She undid the button at the waistband of his trousers, and ran her fingers across his flat abdomen. 'Very nice.'

'*Merci*, Mademoiselle Wynne.' His voice was full of amusement.

She felt the colour flood into her cheeks. 'I didn't mean to say that aloud.'

'I'm glad you did.' He traced a lazy circle round her navel. 'You feel nice, too. Warm and soft. And I'm so going to enjoy exploring you, Amber.'

She was going to enjoy it, too. Given the way he'd danced with her in public, she had a feeling that his private love-making was likely to blow her mind.

She undid his zip, and gently drew the material down to his thighs; his trousers fell to the floor and he stepped out of them, kicking off his shoes and removing his socks as he did so. His erection was very obvious through the soft jersey of his boxer shorts and her mouth went dry.

'Whatever I said earlier, you can still change your mind, *mon ange*,' he said softly.

She shook her head. 'I want you, Guy. It's just…' Her breath hitched. How could she explain?

'I know, *chérie*. It's the same for me. Unexpected.' He

brushed his mouth gently against hers. 'This is just between you and me. Nothing to do with anyone else. No guilt, no worries—just pleasure.'

Pleasure.

Oh, it would be that, all right. For both of them.

He pushed the duvet aside, lifted her up and settled her against the pillows. The white linen was soft and smooth against her skin—seriously expensive high thread-count, she recognised—and the pillows were decadently soft.

Guy hooked his thumbs into the sides of her lacy knickers and gently drew the material down. Amber lifted her bottom slightly to help him remove them; and then she was completely naked in front of him and shyness washed over her.

'I'm going to look at you, *mon ange*,' Guy murmured, correctly reading her expression, 'because you're beautiful. And then I'm going to taste you. And then…' He gave her a lazy grin. 'Then, I'm going to blow your mind.'

'Is that a promise, rather than a threat?' she asked huskily.

'*Absolument.* And—just so you know—I always keep my promises, Amber.'

He teased her nipples with the pad of his thumb; she could feel them tightening and hardening under his touch. Then he leaned forward and took one into his mouth, sucking hard. His mouth was hot against her flesh, making her arch towards him and slide her fingers in his hair. This was good, but she wanted more. Much, much more.

He kissed his way down over her abdomen, and suddenly Amber forgot how to breathe. Was he going to…?

He shifted to kneel between her legs, rocked back on his haunches and gave her a truly wicked grin, one that sent her pulse rocketing. Then he started at her ankle and kissed all the way up; clearly he was paying attention to what made her arch towards him and what made her catch her breath, because he did the same with the other leg.

By the time his mouth was idling along her thigh, she was practically whimpering, her hands fisted in his hair. 'Guy, please…' The words came out as a needy little moan, but it had been months since she'd last had this kind of relief, and nobody had ever made her feel quite this abandoned before.

She felt the long, slow stroke of his tongue along her sex. He swirled the tip round her clitoris, teasing her, and she pushed hard against him, demanding more. He gave her exactly what she needed, varying the pace and pressure so her arousal coiled tighter and tighter and tighter, until she didn't think she could bear it any more. She was babbling his name when her climax exploded through her, more intense than she'd ever thought possible.

This shouldn't have been so good. Not for a first time. It should've been clumsy and embarrassing and faintly disappointing.

But she had a feeling that Guy Lefèvre was no ordinary man.

He shifted up the bed and drew her into his arms, holding her close. 'Better now, *mon ange*?' he asked softly.

She nodded, not trusting herself to speak.

'Good, but that was only the start. To take the edge off.' His eyes were intense. 'Now, it really begins.'

That definitely sounded like a promise.

And Guy had said he was a man who prided himself on keeping his promises.

Almost shyly, she removed his boxer shorts, then sucked in a breath. 'Guy, you're truly beautiful.'

He actually blushed, to her secret pleasure. 'I think that's the first time anyone's told me that.'

She kissed the corner of his mouth. 'And I really,

really want to make love with you.' She stole another kiss. 'Right now.'

He reached over to the drawer in the table next to his bed and removed a foil packet.

She curled her fingers round his. 'My job, I believe.' Gently, she took the condom from him, unwrapped it and rolled it onto him. In response, Guy kissed her hard—and then rolled so that he was lying on his back. He drew her with him so that she was straddling him, and then fitted the tip of his penis to her entrance with one hand and rested the other on her hip, urging her to bear down on him.

God, this felt good. Really, really good.

She moved over him, seeing his eyes darken with pleasure as she lifted and lowered herself; they darkened even more when she tensed her muscles round him.

'Do you like that?' she whispered.

He gave her a slow, sensual smile. 'What do you think, *mon ange*?'

'I think,' she said, 'I want to blow your mind the way you just blew mine.'

'Then do it,' he said, his voice fierce.

She leaned forward to kiss him, nibbling at his lower lip until he opened his mouth and let her deepen the kiss. And then she began to move again, driving them both hard, slowing down so it was like an exquisite torment, then hard again. She could feel her climax rising again, and it shocked her; she'd never come twice so quickly before. Everything in her body seemed to tighten; and, as she hit the peak, she felt his body tense beneath her hands. He sat up and jammed his mouth over hers, kissing her hard as they both came; she held onto him for dear life as wave after wave of sensation swept through her.

Afterwards, he held her close, stroking her hair. 'You have amazing hair. It's the first thing I noticed about you.'

He tangled his fingers in her curls. 'I love these. So soft and silky. And they're natural, yes?'

She nodded. 'I hated it when I was a teenager; my hair would never do what anyone else's did. I even resorted to ironing it, once.'

'Ironing it?'

'That was in the days before you could buy decent hair straighteners. And I kept it straight for quite a while.'

'I'm glad you don't now. This is too glorious to be reined in.' He kissed her swiftly. 'I'd better deal with the condom.'

Which was her cue to leave. 'And I'd better go.'

'Why?' he asked.

'Because it'll be just my luck that I'll bump into someone as I go back to my room, hair all over the place and lipstick kissed away and clothes all crumpled. It'll be so, so obvious what I've just been doing—and, after the way you danced with me tonight, with whom.'

'And that's a problem?'

'Yes.' He'd called her shameless, but she wasn't a tart. 'Look, I know everyone thinks I'm an airhead party girl, but I don't normally sleep with someone until I've known them for a while. And I definitely don't sleep with someone I'm not even dating.'

'There's a way round that,' he said.

Her heart skipped a beat. Was he going to ask her to start dating him?

'Spend the night with me,' he said. 'And we'll get up earlier than everyone else to avoid them. They'll all be exhausted after partying half the night and will sleep in—and those who aren't won't be in the château anyway. They'll be outside in the marquee, waiting for their onion soup.'

'Onion soup? You have to be kidding.'

'The dancing at French weddings goes on until

dawn—and then we have breakfast. Traditionally, in France, it's onion soup—though Allie says she wants to make it Anglo-French and have the option of bacon sandwiches.'

She stared at him in disbelief. 'This has to be the most surreal conversation I've ever had in my life.'

'If I were a true gentleman, *mon ange*,' he said, 'I'd ask you to start dating me. But my life's complicated, right now—I don't need a relationship to make it worse.'

She lifted her chin. 'I don't need a relationship, either. I wasn't fishing.'

'I know you weren't, and I'm making a mess of this.' He sighed. 'Actually, I was hoping to persuade you to come and have a shower with me.'

'A guided tour of your personal bathroom, hmm?'

'A personal tour.' He stole a kiss. 'Very personal.'

'Just so we're clear about it,' she said, 'this is *just* sex, and it's just for tonight, and then it'll be out of our systems, and nobody has to know about it.' And then hopefully she'd be able to look at him without wanting to rip his clothes off.

'That's *a lot* of sex,' he corrected, 'but the rest of it, agreed. It's between you and me.'

'Good.' She licked her lower lip. 'So show me this fabulous bathroom of yours…'

CHAPTER FOUR

AMBER woke, slightly disoriented for a moment; and then the memories of the previous night slammed back in.

She was in bed. Specifically, in Guy Lefèvre's bed. And right now his body was wrapped round hers.

What an idiot she was, jumping into bed with a man she barely knew. Last night's bravado was all gone; this morning, she felt cheap and nasty.

First things first: she needed to wriggle out of his arms, without waking him; find where her clothes were; tiptoe out of his room, still without waking him; and then have a shower and clean her teeth, before facing him.

And then she'd drive herself to the airport.

She could probably skip the 'facing him' step and leave him a note…but that would be even tackier. No, she had to be brave about this. Face up to her mistakes. And hope that somehow *Celebrity Life* wouldn't find out about it and crow about how Bambi had seduced the best man at her friend's wedding. She didn't want Allie and Xav dragged through the mud next to her—or Guy. That wouldn't be fair.

Slowly, carefully, she moved his fingers away from her waist, and then his palm. She'd just freed herself from his arms and wriggled to the side of the bed when she heard him say, *'Bonjour, mon ange.'*

There was nothing she could do now except brazen it out. She sat up and faced him. And oh, he looked good, still rumpled from sleep and with a faint shadowing of stubble. She damped down the surge of desire, knowing how inappropriate it was: they'd agreed that last night was one night only. 'Good morning, Guy. Sorry. I was trying not to wake you.'

'Running out on me?'

'No.' She frowned. 'I was going to have a shower and then face you.'

'You know where my bathroom is.'

Yes—and the shower in which they'd made love last night. Twice. 'That isn't what I meant.' She sighed, sat up and tucked the duvet carefully round her to cover her breasts.

Guy propped himself up on one elbow, looked up at her and laughed.

'What?'

'I think the modest maiden bit might be a little out of place, after last night.'

She felt the colour rush into her face. 'Last night was last night. This morning's different.' She dragged in a breath. 'OK, let's get it over with. I'm sorry for flinging myself at you. I'm trying to break myself of my unsuitable-man habit.'

'But?'

God, he was relentless. 'You were the most gorgeous man at the wedding, and you know it.'

'Actually, I didn't know it,' he corrected, sitting up. 'But thank you for the compliment.'

'If you'd scowled all evening like you did the first time I met you, I could've resisted you.'

'You started it. "Bite me,"' he quoted.

Amber discovered that it was physically possible to blush harder. 'You provoked me.'

'We could agree that we're both as bad as the other,' he suggested.

She sighed. 'Maybe. But, just so you know, I don't usually jump into bed with someone I don't know very well. In fact, you're the first. And I don't want you thinking I'm some kind of cheap—'

He stopped her words very effectively, by leaning over and kissing her swiftly on the mouth. 'You're not cheap. You're high-maintenance.'

'I can maintain myself, thank you very much,' she said, her eyes narrowing. She didn't like where this was going. 'And if you dare offer me—'

He kissed her again to shut her up. 'Why are we fighting?'

'Because you're laughing at me.'

'I'm not laughing at you.' He sighed. 'Are you one of these people who are a complete nightmare in the mornings until you've had a cup of coffee? Because, if you are, I suggest you curl back up under the duvet and I'll go and get you some coffee. And then you don't talk until the caffeine's kicked in.'

'I—' She wasn't. Her friends were all disgusted that Amber could burn the candle quite happily at both ends with no ill effects. It was just *Guy* making her grouchy and out of sorts. Unsettling her.

'Right. Coffee,' he said, and slid out of bed.

He was still completely naked—and unselfconscious about it. Last night, she'd thought he was beautiful. This morning…she still thought he was the most beautiful man she'd ever met. Perfect.

And he'd just said he was going to fetch coffee. Surely he didn't mean…? 'You can't go downstairs naked.'

He shrugged. 'It's my house.'

'Guy—' Her voice came out as a panicky croak. How had she ever thought she could handle a man like this?

And then he grinned. 'You really do need coffee, *mon ange*. I was teasing you. Of course I'm not going downstairs naked. It would hardly be fair to shock the wedding guests.'

But all he did was pull on his trousers—which were obviously creased, as if he'd removed them in a hurry and hadn't bothered hanging them up. Which was, she thought, exactly what had happened. They'd been in such a rush to go to bed with each other that nothing else had mattered except being skin to skin.

He remained barefoot, his hair was rumpled, his face was covered in stubble and he looked utterly louche. Sexy as hell. Desire surged through her entire body, to the point where she almost slid out of bed and started walking towards him.

'Go back to sleep. Coffee's on its way,' he said, and walked out of the room.

No way could she possibly go back to sleep.

She slid out of bed to retrieve her clothes, and groaned. Her dress was impossibly creased. Even a steam cleaner might have problems getting that lot out. And it was her favourite dress. Cross with herself, she hung it carefully over the back of the chair next to Guy's dressing table. And then there was her underwear. She didn't want to put on the clothes she'd worn the day before, so they were out, too. Hopefully Guy would be kind enough to lend her a T-shirt or something, and then she could make a run for it from his room to hers and cross her fingers that nobody came out into the corridor and realised she was wearing nothing at all underneath the T-shirt.

But she'd learned her lesson about making assumptions,

where Guy was concerned; she wasn't going to raid his wardrobe until she'd asked.

In the meantime, there was one thing she could wear to make herself decent. She went into the bathroom, took a towel off the heated rail and tucked it round herself, sarong-style. A glance in the mirror told her that her hair was wild, way beyond control—she'd have to spend a good half an hour combing the knots out. Not to mention using a whole bottle of detangling lotion. She made one attempt at combing through it with her fingers, and winced as she pulled hair from the roots. Not good.

At the same time as she emerged from the bathroom, Guy walked back in with a tray containing a cafetière, two mugs, a jug of milk and a bowl of sugar. 'Very fetching,' he said drily, setting the tray down on his dressing table.

'I don't exactly have a lot of sartorial choice, right now,' she said, scowling.

'Coffee,' he said. 'Please don't talk any more until you've drunk some coffee. Use sign language.'

She did—very pointedly—but he just laughed and ignored it. 'Milk?'

She nodded, bringing her thumb and first finger together to indicate just a tiny amount.

'Sugar?'

A definite shake of the head.

He poured coffee into two mugs, added milk to both and handed one to her. 'Drink, and don't say a word until you're human again.'

She already *was* human. He was the problem, not her. But she subsided and drank her coffee.

'Better?' he asked when she'd finished.

'Not much,' she said, deciding that coming clean was probably the best policy. 'I hate this morning-after awkwardness. I don't know what to say, other than that I'm embarrassed and I feel lousy.'

'If it helps,' he said, 'you don't look lousy.'

She narrowed her eyes at him. 'I wasn't fishing for a compliment. I know perfectly well that my hair's all over the place—and it'll take ages to get all the knots out.'

'Is that what's bothering you?' He placed his mug on the tray and walked into his bathroom. He came out wielding a comb. 'Right. Come and sit here, and I'll get the knots out for you.'

'Thank you for the offer,' she said politely, 'but I'd rather do it myself.'

'Scared I'm going to rip your hair out by the roots?'

'Since you ask, yes. Curly hair is a nightmare. I'll need a ton of detangler to deal with this.'

'I once knew someone like you,' Guy said. 'She had hair exactly like yours. And I learned very quickly how to get knots out of her hair before she started throwing things.'

Amber blinked. 'I don't throw things.' And then the full force of his words hit her. 'You slept with me last night because I look like someone you once dated?' So much for thinking it wasn't possible to feel any worse. Now she felt third-rate, a poor substitute.

'No. I slept with you because you were dancing with the children.'

She shook her head in disbelief. 'You're seriously screwed up.'

He just laughed and patted the bed next to him. 'Come and sit here. I promise I won't hurt you. And you won't need detangler.'

'Yeah, right,' she muttered, but went and sat next to him.

To her surprise, he was incredibly gentle, and she barely felt the pull as he painstakingly combed out the knots.

'You lit up everyone at the wedding last night,' he said softly. 'I was watching you. You weren't flirting with anyone or expecting anyone to wait on you hand and foot. You were making sure that everyone was having a good time. You spent time with the great-aunts and -uncles, making them feel important, and you spent time with the kids, making them feel part of what was going on. Even the shy ones—you made the effort to sit and chat to them. Your warmth is irresistible. *That's* why I slept with you.'

She couldn't say a word; there was a huge lump in her throat.

'That,' he said, 'and the fact that I couldn't get you out of my head for the whole day. Bearing in mind that I've dealt with a few perfume ad campaigns, in my time, I mean it when I say that you're the most stunning woman I've ever seen. And I wanted you, very badly.'

As much as she'd wanted him. With a desperate hunger that had made her act much more recklessly than she usually did—whatever the press might say about her, she didn't usually leap straight into bed with someone she barely knew. This was a first.

'Just so you know.' He dropped a fleeting kiss on her shoulder, and she had to stop herself turning round and sliding her arms round his neck and pressing a kiss to his mouth. Last night was gone. Today was a new day and a new deal.

'OK, your hair's done.'

She moved away, and then turned to face him. 'Thank you. For looking after me just now. And for what you just said.' She dragged in a breath. 'And I'm sorry I was grouchy.'

'*Ça ne fait rien*. So, what now?'

She shrugged. 'I don't know. We said that last night was a one-off.' Even though she was aware that she'd like it to be more than just one night. Guy Lefèvre was full of surprises. Like being able to get the knots out of her hair without hurting her; like the fact he'd noticed what she was good at. Like the fact he wasn't treating her like a cheap tart.

There was something about him. Something she couldn't define, but something that was different from the men she usually dated. He intrigued her. And she wanted to know more.

'So you're going back to England?'

She spread her hands. 'I was originally planning to spend a few days in St Tropez. But Allie's been telling me how gorgeous it is in the Ardèche, so I thought I might take a look around, do the touristy stuff. So if you have any suggestions about places I should visit and good places to stay, now would be a good time. Otherwise I'll check things out on the Internet, and pick somewhere to stay that takes my fancy as I drive round.'

Guy looked at her. This was his cue to suggest somewhere on the far side of the Ardèche. And for him to drive straight back to Grasse and bury himself in work at the perfume house—to put as much distance between them as he could.

But a mad impulse made him say, 'You could stay here.'

'Given what happened last night,' she said carefully, 'is that a good idea?'

No. It wasn't. 'I meant as a base. Not…' Oh, hell. How could he put this without it sounding insulting?

'Message understood,' she said, surprising him. 'But, if I'm going to be your house guest, I hope you'll let me take you out to dinner. In lieu of the fact that I didn't bring a host gift.'

'You don't have to do that.'

'Yes, I do. I'm not a freeloader, you know.'

He blinked. 'I never said you were.'

'Yesterday, you said I was shameless.'

He shrugged. 'You asked me for donations to your charity-ball tombola. How many other people did you ask?'

'That's irrelevant.'

'So you did ask others.'

She lifted her chin. 'It's for a good cause.'

'You're very defensive.'

'Are you surprised?' She sighed. 'Maybe it's not a good idea for me to stay. We'll fight.'

'I'm sorry.'

She looked surprised. 'You're apologising to me?'

He smiled. 'Where we're concerned, it's usually the other way round. Make the most of it.'

'So I can ask you to make it up to me,' she said thoughtfully.

'Name your terms.' He kept his voice light, but his heart rate had speeded up a notch. Was she going to ask for a kiss? And would they end up back between those crumpled sheets, driving each other on to deepest pleasure?

'Could you lend me a T-shirt for about three minutes, please?'

He blinked at the unexpected request. 'A T-shirt?'

She gestured to her dress. 'It's so badly creased, I can't wear it. So, unless you want me to scandalise your guests by running naked from your room to mine, I need something to wear. Look, I'll wash and iron it before I return it, if you like.'

He laughed. 'I bet you've never ironed a thing in your life.'

'I'm not lazy.'

'I know.' He touched her cheek with the backs of his

fingers. 'You helped out in the kitchen, the night of the barbecue. But you don't iron, do you?'

'All right, I use a laundry service. And I have someone come in to clean for me.' She put her hands on her hips and glared at him. 'Satisfied?'

He raised an eyebrow. 'I'm just wondering what a party girl does all day.' Did she spend her days the way that Véra had?

Her eyes narrowed. 'I have lunch with my friends, I go shopping and I giggle while we paint each other's nails.'

'Nope. Apart from the fact that you don't giggle, I think you'd be bored doing just that.'

'So what do you think I do all day?' she challenged.

'I think you spend half the week planning and schmoozing and talking people into doing things for your charity stuff, and the other half going out to lunch, the cinema and the theatre with your friends. Oh, and partying, of course.'

She spread her hands. 'Busted. Though I do like shopping. Especially for shoes,' she added. 'So may I borrow a T-shirt, please?'

'I think seeing you wearing just a T-shirt would put any male around here in heart failure,' Guy said, heading for the bathroom. He took his bathrobe from the back of the door. 'Try this.'

She took it, smiling gratefully at him.

'And you don't have to wash it before you give it back,' he added with a grin.

She gave him a speaking look—then, to his surprise, she stood up, untucked the towel and dropped it.

He was definitely having trouble breathing when she gave him a seriously saucy grin, then shrugged on his bathrobe and tied the belt round her waist. 'That's what you get for being cheeky,' she said.

A surge of desire rendered him temporarily speechless, and by the time he'd thought up a suitable retort she'd kissed him lightly on the cheek, scooped up her clothes and vanished—leaving the towel defiantly on the floor.

He sat back on the bed. Amber Wynne intrigued him and annoyed him in equal measures. She was a party girl and a spoiled media darling—and yet there was more to her than that. And last night had felt like nothing he'd ever known. That mad, hot, sweet intensity, the way she'd responded to his touch, the way she'd explored him and found out just what drove him wild...

If things were different, he'd definitely be dating her. Though he'd be taking it much, much more slowly than they had last night.

He must have been out of his mind, offering to let her stay here. How the hell was he going to sleep, knowing that she was at the other end of the corridor? He didn't even have the comfort of his lab to distract him, right now: only the endless search for someone who could help him fix the problem. A search that he was beginning to think might be fruitless, and the idea that he might never be able to work again at the job he loved so much ripped him to shreds. What use was a parfumier who couldn't smell? He'd have to do something else. Sure, he was capable of turning his hand to something else, but his heart wouldn't be involved any more. So it wouldn't be living: it would be mere existence.

What was that old Chinese curse? *May you live in interesting times.*

The next few days were certainly going to be interesting.

CHAPTER FIVE

WRAPPED in Guy's fluffy navy bathrobe, Amber could smell his citrussy scent all the way to her room; it was as if his arms were wrapped round her and her face were pillowed against his chest, the way it had been last night. Comforting.

And that in itself was scary. Since when did she need a man to comfort her or make her feel protected?

She really couldn't work Guy out. He owned the château and a perfume house, so he was financially on equal terms with the men she usually dated—but he wasn't like them. He didn't have that hard edge. She couldn't pigeonhole him as a financier who liked dancing until dawn or a lawyer who liked the best tables at the best restaurants.

Guy Lefèvre had a lot more facets to him, and maybe that was what was throwing her. What was drawing her to him.

He was a generous lover and he had a huge reservoir of kindness; he'd been patient enough to work all the knots out of her hair this morning without complaint and without hurting her. Yet he was also the man who'd been so angry with her in the rose garden for picking a single rose. The same man who'd made it very clear that he wasn't looking for a relationship; and yet he'd offered to let her stay here while she was looking round the area.

As a base, not…

Yeah, she knew. She was the kind of girl that men wanted to snog but not marry. A good-time party girl. And that was fine, because she didn't particularly want to get married and settle down. Or, if she did, it'd be to someone from her own world. Her parents were a shining example of what not to do: they'd been from totally different worlds and they'd been really unhappy together. But when her father had remarried—to a lawyer, someone who understood the business circles he moved in—he'd become settled and happy. Her mother, who was on her fourth husband, was rather less so; or maybe that was just Hollywood, Amber thought, because celeb marriages were lived so much in the spotlight that they often couldn't handle the strain.

Pushing the thoughts from her head, Amber showered swiftly, moisturised her skin, put her hair back in a pony-tail, and changed into black jeans and a hot-pink strappy top. She had the perfect shoes: shiny, platform-soled stilettos in the same colour as her top, with the tiniest strap around her ankle. A spritz of Chanel No 5 and a touch of sheer lipstick, and she was ready to face the world.

And if anyone said anything about her disappearing act last night…well, she'd just give an enigmatic smile. With a smile, you could get through anything.

Guy had said something about breakfast for the wedding guests in the marquee. She still wasn't sure whether he'd been teasing her, but if it turned out that he had she could always bluff it and say she'd wanted some fresh air.

As soon as she rounded the corner of the garden, she knew he'd been telling the truth. About the onion soup, too; several guests were tucking into bowls of the stuff.

Xav and Allie were there, still in their wedding finery; though Amber was relieved to see that neither of them was eating soup.

'We all thought you'd be the last one standing. What happened to you last night?' Allie teased.

The man sitting at your table happened to me, Amber thought; but wild horses wouldn't drag the admission from her. The way Guy was dressed, he looked even more gorgeous than he had the previous night. Faded, soft denims and a black cashmere sweater—and he looked utterly touchable. It was all she could do not to march over and grab him and jam her mouth over his.

'Bambi?' Allie looked worried. 'Are you all right?'

'Bit of a headache.' That was real enough. 'Too much champagne,' she fibbed.

Allie looked relieved. 'Sounds like you need a bacon sandwich.'

'Cake would be better. The best hangover cure ever is cake,' Amber said.

'You're telling me that you eat cake for *breakfast*?' Guy asked, looking shocked.

She wasn't going to let him see that he rattled her. Right now, she was Bambi Wynne, Party Girl, and she was going to do what she did best: she was going to *shine*. 'Leftover pudding is even better. If you haven't had pavlova or chocolate bread-and-butter pudding for breakfast, you haven't lived.'

Guy raised his eyebrow. 'So that makes us all zombies, does it?'

'Speak for yourself, sweetie.' She blew him a kiss. 'I'm going to get myself some coffee.'

'No need. There's a jug here.' To her shock, he shifted over and made room for her.

Sitting next to him would scramble her brains. But refusing to sit there would make everyone else ask questions. Caught between a rock and a hard place, she thought ruefully, and sat next to him.

He took a clean mug from the tray in the middle of the table, and poured coffee into it for her. 'I don't know how you like it,' he said.

Her eyes met his. Liar. He knew exactly how she liked it.

Coffee *and* sex.

Without missing a beat, he added, 'So help yourself to milk.'

'*Merci*, Monsieur Guy,' she said sweetly, and shifted her foot so she could press her heel into his toe.

'That's going to cost you later,' he murmured, *sotto voce*, before adding in a louder tone, 'So you seriously eat pudding for breakfast?'

'She reads menus backwards, too,' Allie said. 'There was one occasion when she met me for lunch—I was trying to persuade her to come and do event management for me, so I went along with what she ordered. Except she ordered two puddings and no main course.'

Amber spread her hands. 'What can I say? I have a sweet tooth.'

'But you don't take sugar in your coffee?' Guy asked. 'That's contradictory.'

'Don't be mean, Guy,' Xavier said. 'Amber, just ignore my little brother. He's a nerdy scientist with no social skills.'

'Says the nerdy vigneron whose wife needs to teach him some social skills,' Guy retorted with a grin.

When the waiter came over with a pile of bacon sandwiches, Guy said something swiftly that Amber couldn't catch to translate. If he'd ordered her a bowl of onion soup, she thought, it'd end up in his lap.

Two minutes later, the waiter reappeared with a bowl of lemon tart and a jug of cream. 'Mademoiselle?' he said with a smile. '*Pour vous.*'

Guy said nothing, though his eyes had crinkled round the corners. And it warmed her that he'd gone to the trouble to ask for this for her.

'*Merci,*' she said to the waiter. 'And thank you, too, Guy.'

He'd been calling her bluff. But she amazed him by eating every scrap, with gusto. His ex-wife had never touched puddings, or anything else containing carbs, and she'd counted every single gram of fat; whereas Amber had poured cream quite happily over the lemon tart.

He really couldn't work Amber out. She appeared dedicated purely to pleasure. She'd even turned down an offer of working with Allie—which he found odd, because event management would've suited Amber very well. Organising things and charming people, with a smiley public face: they were all her strengths. She could've made a fantastic career out of it, and yet she chose to organise events for nothing. For fun. Though she'd admitted to him last night that it was also for a cause very close to her heart, so clearly there was a serious side to her. One that he had a feeling she kept hidden from most people.

And then there were her shoes.

When she'd come strutting round the corner, in those crazy shoes, he'd wanted to leave the table, scoop her up and carry her back to his bed, the way he'd done the previous night.

Having her stay here wasn't going to be good for his blood pressure. Or his peace of mind. If they hadn't been surrounded by wedding guests, he wouldn't have been able to resist bending his head and licking off that tiny smear of cream on the corner of her mouth.

Oh, for pity's sake. Hadn't he learned from his mistakes with Véra? Clearly not, because Amber was from the same world. Celebrity parties, premières, her life lived through the camera lens and splashed across magazines. As a nerdy scientist, Guy hadn't fitted into that scene. At all. He'd loathed the intrusiveness of the gossip pages and the paparazzi—so what was he doing, letting himself dally with someone who was perfectly at home with that kind of attention and probably even courted it?

He needed to put the brakes on, right now.

'That was perfect,' Amber said. She smiled, and leaned back in her chair. 'The perfect pleasure. And life is all about pleasure.'

'That might be a good name for your new perfume, Guy,' Xavier said. 'Pleasure.'

The name of Guy's perfume was still under wraps, even from his brother and his business partner. And how strange that the pet name he'd found himself calling Amber was so close to it. 'I'm still thinking about the name,' Guy said lightly.

'Joy would be good, too,' Amber added.

Guy shook his head. 'That name was taken back in nineteen thirty.'

'Really?' She looked surprised.

'Patou's Joy is one of the most famous, uplifting fragrances ever. It's a great name, but I can't rip it off.'

'Don't argue with him, Amber,' Allie said. 'He has an encyclopaedic memory and can tell you who designed the scent, what all the notes are and probably who designed the bottle.'

'Well, hey. I wouldn't be much of a parfumier if I couldn't.' And he probably wouldn't be one for much longer. Guy forced himself to damp down the fear. Not now, not here. Wait until he was in his lab and wouldn't be disturbed. Then he could check the Internet and see if any new research had turned up in the last two days. See if anyone was running any kind of medical trials, maybe, where he would be a suitable candidate for treatment. There had to be something. Science moved on all the time. He wasn't the only one in the world who'd suffered from anosmia; someone, somewhere, would be investigating the problem and someone, somewhere, would have answers. He just had to find that one person and everything would be all right again.

After breakfast, Allie and Xavier changed and left for Paris; everyone waved them off from the front of the château. During the morning, the rest of the wedding guests drifted away, and workmen came to take down the marquee. Guy had disappeared too, so, after making coffee for herself and the team dealing with the marquee, Amber sat at the table on the terrace overlooking the garden, armed with paper, a pen and her mobile phone, and began looking up local beauty spots on the Internet.

An hour later, Guy emerged from his lab to make himself a coffee. Looking through the kitchen window, he could see Amber ensconced on the terrace, making notes of some kind. Might as well make her a drink at the same time, he thought, and carried a mug out to her.

She was definitely making notes; but what amused him was that she was clearly replying to a stream of texts with her left hand while she wrote notes with her right. Definitely a multi-tasker, then. And he'd just bet that all the texts were from her party-girl friends. And that they'd all be written in textspeak—something he loathed utterly.

Deciding not to disturb her, he placed the mug of coffee next to her in silence; but she looked up and smiled at him, sending a rush of heat through his body.

'Thanks, that's really kind of you,' she said.

'*Ça ne fait rien*. It's possibly a bit too cool to use the pool, but feel free if you want to.'

'Thanks.' She gave him another of those smiles, and he had to stop himself wondering what she'd look like in the pool, with her hair spread out around her. Like a mermaid, probably. Sexy as hell, with that kissable mouth pouting up at him.

He stared at the floor, trying to get his thoughts back under control. Bad move. She was still wearing those ridiculous shoes. They were completely impractical. And he couldn't get them out of his head. Or the thoughts of what her feet looked like out of those shoes. How her legs went on for ever. How her legs had felt, wrapped round his body.

'I'll try not to get in your way while I'm staying here,' she said.

She could try, but he had a nasty feeling that it wouldn't make any difference. And an even nastier feeling that even if she weren't staying at the château, he'd still be thinking about her. There was something about her that drew him, caught his attention. 'What are you doing?'

'Planning where I'm going.' She showed him the list. 'What do you think?'

He read it swiftly. The lake at Issarles, the Pont d'Arc, the gorges and the Ray-Pic waterfall. All favourite tourist spots—and some of the most beautiful places on earth. 'You'll enjoy them.'

'Anything else you can think of? The main produce here is wine, yes?'

'And chestnuts, olives and lavender.'

She scribbled more notes. 'Any local specialty foods I should try? Well, obviously apart from chestnuts?'

'Picodon cheese.'

'Right.' She looked thoughtful. 'That dinner I owe you—can it be somewhere they do local dishes?'

'You don't owe me dinner.'

She flapped a dismissive hand. 'We've already argued that and I won.'

She most definitely hadn't won, but he could see that she was set on it. Arguing would get him nowhere. 'When were you thinking?'

'Tonight.'

And he'd need a long, cold shower first, to make sure he kept his hands off her. Especially if she was wearing those shoes. 'I'll book a table. I have things to do this afternoon.'

'Cool. Meet you at your front door at seven? And I'll drive.'

'I'll drive,' he corrected.

'In your monster four-by-four?' she scoffed. 'My hire car's more fun.'

'The four-by-four was Xav's car. I'll bet you mine's more fun than yours.'

'A bet, hmm? What are the stakes?'

For a second, he couldn't breathe.

A kiss.

And he could see the same thought reflected in her eyes. A kiss. His lips parting hers. His tongue duelling against hers. Her naked body pressed against his. Losing himself in her warm, sweet depths.

'No stakes,' he muttered hoarsely. 'Just saying.'

Her phone rang; she looked at it and smiled. 'I'd better answer that. *Ciao*, babe.' She gave him a tiny dismissive wave and then, with incredible insouciance, pressed a button on her phone and started chatting—as if nothing had happened between them just then.

She was going to drive him crazy.

And he really needed that cold shower.

He needed it even more when he saw his bathrobe folded neatly on his bed. Unable to help himself, he brought the material up to his face. Breathed in, even though he knew damn well that he wouldn't be able to smell her scent.

And he was definitely going crazy, because he could've sworn that he smelled roses. A scent that broke his heart.

Dinner.

It had to be a little black dress, then. Even though this wasn't a date, Amber still intended to dress up for it. The pink shoes? No. Too obvious. In the end, she decided to go for the classic look: the black dress, a pair of plain black stilettos and a black pearl choker. She put her hair up again with the white pearl-headed pins—which she'd rescued from Guy's bedroom when she returned his bathrobe—and added a smudge of charcoal eyeliner and a slick of a slightly darker lipstick, for evening wear. She studied her reflection in the mirror. Excellent. She looked businesslike. And this was business, of a sort. *Not* a date.

When she met Guy in the hall, she had to swallow hard. He was dressed in smart-casual, black trousers teamed with a smoky blue cashmere sweater that really brought out the colour of his eyes. His hair looked slightly rumpled, as if he'd been in his mysterious lab and had raked his hair out of his eyes while he was working; and it made her remember how he'd looked this morning, all rumpled and sexy and wearing only a pair of trousers.

Oh, help.

Last night had been a one-off. She was officially off men.

But she knew that all he'd have to do would be crook his little finger and she'd be wrapped right round him, kissing him until they were both dizzy.

She really had to get a grip.

She blinked when he opened the front door for her and she walked out of the château to see the car parked on the gravel drive. Low-slung, sleek and gorgeous, with a soft top.

'Like it?' Guy asked as he opened the passenger door.

'It's OK.'

'Going to admit it's better than yours?'

She sighed. 'All right. It's better. Though it's a bit flash for you.'

He laughed. 'This is my solitary vice.' Then he gave her a sidelong look as he got into the car. 'Well, one of them. I don't have that many.'

Her mouth went dry. She'd found out what one of them was, last night. Something he was seriously good at. And she wished her dress were made of thicker material when her nipples responded to the memory. He couldn't fail to notice.

Well, two could play at flirting. She fluttered her eyelashes. 'I'm not sure I dare ask what the others are.'

'The car's number one. This—' he switched on the stereo, and loud rock music filled the car '—is number two.'

'Dinosaur rock?' She'd had him pegged as a classical fan.

'And number three is—' he paused, until she met his eyes '—off limits.'

Oh, double help.

He knew exactly what he was doing.

Well, if that was the way he wanted to play it… She shifted in her seat so her hemline rose up a bit. And she knew she'd hit the target when he whacked up the volume on the stereo to hide his intake of breath.

He turned it down again when they were on the road out of the village. 'Sorry. Bad habit, listening to loud music. And I guess it wouldn't be your kind of thing.'

'I don't mind this. You can at least sing along with it,' she said.

'Getting middle-aged?' he teased.

'I'm only four months older than you.'

When he said nothing, she glanced at him. 'What?'

'How do you know how old I am?'

'I looked you up on Google. So I also know that you won a huge award at a ridiculously young age, developed a couple of top-selling perfumes for a big name in the perfume industry and then set up your own perfume house, also at a ridiculously young age.' She paused. It had been niggling her all afternoon. And he had to know that if she'd looked him up on the Internet, his divorce would've been one of the biggest stories about him. So there was no point in pussyfooting round it. 'And that you used to be married to a supermodel.'

'Right.'

'She has straight hair, nowadays. And it's blonde. Nothing like mine.'

'Is it?'

Was he really as unbothered as he sounded? Or was that all an act, as she suspected? She sighed. 'I suppose I should be flattered. Or is that why you don't like me?'

'I didn't say I don't like you.'

'You don't have to *say* it.' The way they ended up sniping at each other, it was all too obvious. 'I guess, from the back, we might have looked a bit alike—that's why you were grouchy with me in your rose garden, isn't it?'

Guy blew out a breath. 'Do we have to have this conversation?'

'Yes. Because, actually, I'm a bit annoyed at the thought that you slept with me because of her.'

'I didn't sleep with you because of her.'

'No?' she said. 'You told me you knew someone with

hair like that and she threw things. That's how you learned how to get knots out of hair without detangler spray.'

'You don't look that much like her, not facially,' Guy said. 'Though you're from the same world as her.'

'Which is why you don't want to date me.'

'One of the reasons, yes. It's not my world. I'm not interested in making small talk, or gossiping about other people's love lives. And I don't enjoy living in a goldfish bowl where everything's out of proportion and the unimportant stuff takes over.'

While he had been married to a supermodel, he would certainly have been a target for the paparazzi, she thought. But there was more to her world than just gossip. Then she realised what he'd said first. 'So what are the other reasons?' she asked, suddenly curious.

'I thought you didn't want to date me, either?'

'I don't, because you'd probably think it's only because I know you're loaded and I'd expect you to shower me with expensive presents.' She lifted her chin. 'Just so you know, I have my own flat in London and a trust fund. I pay my own way. And I don't expect men to shower me with presents. Though, if they want to, vice number four is acceptable.'

'Shoes?'

'Chocolate,' she corrected. 'But it has to be *good* chocolate.'

'Just out of interest,' Guy said, sounding incredibly casual, 'why would you want to date me?'

'Shared vices,' she said. 'Specifically, number one.'

'I would've said number three.' Guy's voice was just that little bit deeper.

Suddenly, there wasn't enough air in the car. And she could still remember how he'd felt inside her. How he'd made her feel. All that power, channelled right in on her, pushing her closer and closer to the edge—and holding her as she fell.

She couldn't cope with this. 'Any chance of having the roof down?' She really hoped he couldn't hear the quiver in her voice.

'On a late-September evening?'

'Yes.' Because it would be cold enough to freeze out the hot surge of desire. And it might blow some common sense back into her head.

'Sure.' He pressed a button, and the top folded up.

Between the noise of the road, the noise of the wind and the sound of his stereo, there was no hope of having a conversation. Which was a good thing, Amber decided. She'd already said way too much for comfort, this evening.

What was it about him that threw her like this?

Guy parked outside an unpromising-looking place, put the hood back up and turned off the stereo. The moment that they walked inside the restaurant and Amber smelled the scent of the food, she knew he'd picked somewhere good. 'This place smells gorgeous,' she said.

Was it her imagination, or did he just flinch?

Her imagination, she decided, because then he shrugged.

'The food's pretty good.' And he'd clearly been here before, because the waiter greeted him by name. 'What would you like to drink, Amber?'

'Something soft, please.'

He spread his hands. 'I'm driving, so it's safe for you to drink.'

'I might be a party girl,' Amber said, 'but I do keep an eye on my liver. Sparkling water is just fine, thank you. With a slice of orange, please.'

'Not lemon or lime?' He looked slightly amused. 'Oh,

wait. You have a sweet tooth. And I bet number four means white chocolate.'

'Don't be smart.'

He grinned. 'It does, doesn't it?'

'Actually,' she told him loftily, 'it's gianduja, praline, for your information. Which, for your information, is better than number three.'

'Is it, now? Interesting theory.'

It was on the tip of her tongue to tell him that she could prove it, but she knew he was waiting for her to say that. Instead, she said sweetly, 'Perhaps you'd be kind enough to ask for the menus as well as the water?'

'There isn't actually a menu here. They serve what the chef feels like cooking.'

'That's fine. I don't mind going with the flow.' She gave him a pointed look. 'I'm not one of these people who makes a fuss about every course and insists that things are changed to make myself feel important.' Though she'd just bet that his ex had. And, given that she came from the same kind of world as her, she'd bet that he was judging her by his ex's standards. Which wasn't fair.

And it was time they changed the subject. In her experience, the best way of drawing someone out was to ask them about themselves. Given that what he did for a living wasn't a run-of-the-mill job, he was bound to open up to her if she asked about his work. 'So what made you choose perfumery as a career?' she asked.

No doubt she was just being polite, Guy thought, but she'd unerringly picked the one subject that could really rattle him. His career. Soon to be ex-career, if he couldn't find a doctor to help him. 'I was always good at chemistry at school—and I'm interested in how scent works, how it can change perceptions and moods.'

'And you're wearing your signature scent tonight—Bergamote Fraîche?'

'Looked that up on Google as well, did you?' he asked.

'No. I noticed it yesterday.' She blushed slightly, and Guy knew exactly where she'd noticed it. On his skin, while she'd been kissing him. His body tightened at the memory.

'Gina said that *Celebrity Life* raved about your citrussy shower gel—' she rolled her eyes '—which has to be about the only nice thing it's done all year. And Allie said it was an extension of the line; it was the first cologne you created for GL Parfums.'

Yes. And he might just have created his very last fragrance. He forced himself not to tense up, and drawled, 'You've done your homework.' Then he thought about what she'd just said. 'What did you mean about being the only nice thing *Celebrity Life* has done all year?'

She flapped a dismissive hand. 'Nothing.'

'The magazine's run stories about you?'

'Which I ignore.'

'You could get an injunction.' He could remember Véra doing that with one particular magazine.

'If I did, they'd report that, too—with glee,' Amber said with a sigh. 'The magazine never tells outright lies, so I can't take them to court. It's the spin they put on the facts.' She shrugged. 'Guess I'll have to live with it. I never read that magazine, anyway. Though the stories end up spreading through the others.'

'Doesn't it bother you?'

'It used to,' she admitted, 'but then I thought about it. When people have had a rough day at work, they can come home and relax with a magazine, read all about the lovely things that their favourite celebs are wearing or have just bought for their home, and find out where they can get the same look for a fraction of the price on the high street. Who am I to stop them having that pleasure?'

He hadn't considered things from that viewpoint. He'd just thought about the intrusiveness; and Véra had been furious when a magazine had taken a picture of her at a party and done exactly that kind of feature on her. She'd always worn very exclusive clothes given to her by designers.

'Do the paparazzi stalk you?' he asked, thinking of the way he'd been doorstepped when news broke of the split between himself and Véra.

'Now and again. And they're going to run a lulu of a story about me this week,' she said, rolling her eyes. 'I went to Venice last week to pick up Allie and Xav's wedding present—these gorgeous Venetian wine glasses. Someone snapped me falling flat on my face as I stepped into the water taxi by the airport and lost my footing. I saw the flash as I hit the floor.' She shrugged. 'Never mind. They got a nice shot of my shoes. And if they do run it, I might ring *What's Hot!* magazine—that's *Celebrity Life*'s biggest rival—and tell them where I got the shoes. One of Gina's friends from art school became a shoe designer, and her shoes are just gorgeous. If they give her a puff, it'll be really good for her sales.'

'And then she'll give you free shoes?' That was the way he remembered it working.

She gave him a scornful look. 'Of course not. If Zaza kept me in free shoes, she'd go bankrupt! I already told you, Guy, I pay my way.'

'I didn't mean to offend you.' But it intrigued him that she saw things in such a different way. 'You're very relaxed about the press.' Even about the prospect of having a photograph of her in less than a flattering light splashed across the magazines. Véra would've stormed round the house in a fury for days. Or was Amber simply putting a brave face on things, the same way that he was right now?

'I used to get uptight, when I was a teenager, but Mum sat me down and said that if you kept smiling, you were the one in control.' She took a sip of her mineral water. 'So that's what I do. I keep smiling. The more the stress, the bigger my smile.'

Amber turned out to be incredibly easy to talk to; Guy found himself talking to her about all kinds of things, from the sort of books he enjoyed reading through to the fact he missed having a dog but it wasn't fair to have one when he spent so much time in his lab, splitting his time between Grasse and the château. And it turned out that she liked dogs, too, but didn't have one as it wouldn't be fair to keep one cooped up in her London flat. He discovered that they liked the same kind of films, too. And she was a fellow foodie; unlike Véra, she didn't nibble on a lettuce leaf or claim she was full after one mouthful. She ate with gusto, commenting on textures and seasonings and how they worked together.

He couldn't quite work her out. Just when he thought he'd pigeonholed her, she said or did something that threw him. One minute, she was the spoiled media darling, working the press to her best advantage; and then she revealed unexpected depths. Then, just when he was beginning to think that there was a lot more to her, she said or did something that reminded him so much of his ex-wife that he almost started grinding his teeth.

But she also intrigued him more than anyone had in years.

What was it about her?

'Allie said she tried to persuade you to do event management for her. Why did you turn her down?' he asked.

'Because I don't want to be tied down to someone else's

schedule. Organising the charity balls and helping friends organise parties is fun. And I can still do what I like, most of the time. I can enjoy having lunch with my friends without having to worry that I'll be late back for work, and I can go and see my mum in LA without having to book time off weeks in advance and then come back to London before I'm really ready to leave. I like my life as it is.' She eyed the remaining chocolate on the plate between them. 'I suppose, as you're my dinner guest, I ought to be nice and offer that to you.'

'As I'm your guest, I'll be polite and refuse so you can have it.' He couldn't resist teasing her. 'Are you sure chocolate's only number four on your list of vices?'

She blushed spectacularly. 'Don't be mean.'

Then she had her revenge. Because she ate the chocolate really *slowly*. Just like the model in one of the confectionary ads that had stirred him as a teenager. Her mouth was practically having sex with the chocolate, and Guy couldn't take his eyes off her. By the time she'd finished, he was near to hyperventilating.

And he knew that she knew exactly what effect she'd had on him, because she gave him the sauciest smile. 'I'll go and pay.'

'No, it's my bill.'

'The deal was,' she corrected crisply, 'that you'd allow me to take you out to dinner as a thank you for letting me stay at the château. But I might need your help if I get stuck on the language. I'll call you over if I do.'

No, she wouldn't need his help, he thought. She'd smile and mime her way through it, and have all the restaurant staff smiling along with her. She charmed everyone she met; the waiter had loved it when she'd made the effort to speak to him in French and complimented him on the meal and the service, even though her grammar and her accent weren't perfect and she had to ask for help with some of the words.

She charmed him, too. Even though he knew he ought to be wary of getting involved with someone from her world, her sunny, bright, super-optimistic outlook was infectious—and he was finding her seriously hard to resist.

He relaxed more on the drive back to the château, this time switching the stereo to a classical station.

'This is more the kind of stuff that I thought you'd listen to,' Amber said.

'I do when I'm working.' He glanced at her. 'Do you want the roof down again?'

'No need. I've had chocolate.'

He couldn't help laughing. 'Number four being a substitute for number three?'

'Don't knock it. There are surveys out there that prove women prefer chocolate to sex. It's all to do with satiation centres in the brain.' When he said nothing, she said, 'OK, so I dropped out of university, but it wasn't because I was thick.'

That was clearly a sore spot. Had people accused her of being an airhead? 'Anyone who talks to you will know you're not stupid. What were you reading?'

'History of art. And, as I didn't want to go and work in a gallery, it all felt a bit pointless. Better that the place went to a student who really wanted to do it,' she said.

'Fair enough.'

'That isn't what Dad said.' She shrugged. 'But he came round in the end. After I threatened to become a model, he stopped nagging me about getting a proper job.'

A model. Like Véra. Guy went cold. 'Did you want to be a model?' he asked carefully.

'And exist on lettuce leaves for years? No chance. I like food.'

'You're slender enough to get away with eating what you like—and I've seen how much pudding you eat.'

'I still wouldn't do it. It's not a nice world—people watch you and wait for you to fail. And there's so much jealousy and backstabbing.' She grimaced. 'No, thanks. That's no fun.'

'And your life's all about fun.'

'Exactly. Not that I expect *you* to get that.'

'Because I'm boring?' he asked, thinking of the accusations that his ex-wife had flung at him.

'No, because you're über-clever. You're a scientist. You're looking for different things out of life.'

She'd hit the nail squarely on the head, he thought. They were from different worlds. In his life with Véra, Guy had hated the media spotlight, the first nights and celeb cocktail parties where he was expected to make small talk with people he had nothing in common with; whereas Amber, like Véra, would thrive on them. She loved parties and meeting new people, and she treated everyone she met as a potential new friend; her warmth wore down any barriers. They were complete opposites; so there was no point in starting something that would never work. No matter how tempting he found her. And they'd agreed that last night was last night.

So it had to end here.

CHAPTER SIX

AMBER excused herself when they got back to the château, saying that she was a bit tired. Guy had a feeling that she wasn't telling the truth, but he didn't call her on it. Instead, he sat up in his lab, checking the Internet for any new developments in the treatment of anosmia, the loss of sense of smell.

Even though his eyes were aching by the time he'd finished, he couldn't settle. He wasn't sure whether it was more because of the fact he hadn't found anything new, or because he knew Amber was asleep upstairs and part of him was regretting that he hadn't taken the chance to change things between them, start seeing her properly. Despite the fact that his life wasn't in the right place for a relationship, something about her made his world feel brighter. Part of him really wanted to take the chance; and yet part of him knew that it would be unfair to use her in that way. It was already bad enough that he'd slept with her last night and let her help him forget his worries. Selfish as hell.

'You're a mess, Lefèvre,' he told himself. 'And you need sleep.' Maybe in the morning everything would seem different.

At the foot of the stairs, he realised that the light was on in the kitchen. He must've left it on, earlier. He walked in, intending to switch it off, and discovered Amber there, hunched over at the table.

'Are you all right?' he asked.

'I couldn't sleep,' she admitted. 'I just made myself some hot milk and cinnamon.'

'Cinnamon.' He couldn't smell it right now, but he could remember the scent. Heady. Like her.

'Sorry, I know I should've asked first. I hope you don't mind that I poked about in your kitchen.'

'Not a problem. Help yourself,' he said.

Her eyes narrowed as she looked at him. 'Are you all right?'

'Yes,' he lied.

'You look as if you've spent too long in front of a computer screen. Your eyes are bloodshot.'

'I couldn't sleep, either,' he admitted.

She handed him the mug. 'Try this.'

He took a sip, more to humour her than anything else; his sense of taste was going along with his sense of smell. 'So why can't you sleep?'

There was a long, long pause. He said nothing, waiting for her to speak; finally, she sighed. 'Number three.'

He was impressed that she'd had the courage to admit it. And fair was fair. 'Me, too,' he said softly. 'Maybe I should call my new perfume that.'

'Is that what your new perfume's about?'

'No.' But he knew exactly what fragrance he wanted to make next. A hypnotic, sensual one with a glossy surface and a hidden depth of sweetness. Like her. And it frustrated him to hell that he couldn't do it. All the notes of the perfume were in his head, and part of him wanted to run to his lab and start creating it: but he knew there was no point. Not until his nose was fixed. Until then, he wouldn't be able to check if the formula needed tweaking.

He couldn't do anything about that, right now. But the other problem—the attraction between himself and Amber—was something he could sort out. 'So what are we going to do about this?' he asked her.

'I don't know. But I don't think it's a good idea for me to stay here with you.' She took the mug back from him and sipped. 'Especially if you're going to wear touchable clothes. Because I'm a bit impulsive and I don't always know when to stop.' She dragged in a breath. 'It's OK for you. You have a sensible job and a sensible life and a sensible outlook.'

'Not always. Especially when the most beautiful woman I've ever met decides to hike her skirt up in my car.' He looked at her. 'Are you wearing anything at all under that silky wrap?' It was hot pink, like her sexy shoes—though right at that moment she was barefoot.

'I don't think I should answer that.'

He groaned. 'I think you just did.'

'It's OK. I'm going upstairs to have a very, very cold shower. And I'm moving out to a hotel tomorrow.'

'No.' He reached out and took her hand, drawing it up to his lips. 'I know this is a seriously bad idea, but I don't think either of us is going to get any sleep at all tonight if we don't do something about this—' he paused, shaking his head in frustration because he couldn't think of the right word '—this *thing* between us.' Even though she was the kind of girl he'd sworn he'd never go near again, he simply couldn't resist her. He needed to taste her. Needed to feel her skin against his. Needed the release that only she could give him.

Her eyes looked absolutely enormous. 'So what are you suggesting? That we have a mad affair?'

'One night didn't get it out of our systems,' he said. 'Maybe it just takes a little longer than that.'

'But it's not going to be serious.'

'Agreed. Exclusive, though,' he warned, remembering his ex.

'Definitely.' She dragged in a breath. 'Starting now?'

'Oh, *Dieu*, yes,' he said, wrapping his arms round her and doing what he'd been thinking about all evening— jamming his mouth over hers. And her mouth was warm and sweet and sexy as hell. So were her hands, sliding under his sweater and stroking his skin.

'My room,' she said as he broke the kiss.

'You're on,' he said, scooping her up and carrying her up the stairs.

When Guy woke in Amber's bed, the following morning, he was slightly disoriented at first; and then disconcerted to find that he was alone in the bed. The coolness of the sheets where she'd lain suggested that he'd been alone for a few minutes. He could see the en suite from the bed, so he knew she wasn't in the shower.

'Amber?'

No reply.

Frowning, he climbed out of bed, pulled on his under- pants and trousers, and headed downstairs.

She was back in the kitchen. Barefoot again, and wear- ing only her silky wrap.

And he knew for a fact that she wore nothing underneath it.

How to make a man's blood pressure spike.

He stood in the doorway, watching her potter about. She was humming to herself as she whisked something in a bowl, completely absorbed in whatever she was making. She looked adorable, and it took a lot of effort for him not to go over to her, turn her round to face him and kiss her until both their heads were spinning.

'*Bonjour, mon ange,*' he said from the doorway.

She turned round and smiled at him, making his heart skip a beat. '*Bonjour*, Guy. I was going to bring you breakfast in bed but, since you're up, have a seat.' She smiled again. 'I'm making pancakes.'

He blinked. 'You eat crêpes for breakfast in England?'

'No, but my mum does in LA. Anyway, these are American breakfast pancakes. Thicker and fluffier. We're having them with stewed apples and Chantilly cream.'

She'd taken him at his word last night, then, and made herself at home in his kitchen, finding the ingredients and utensils she needed.

But pancakes for breakfast? Considering she'd eaten lemon tart with cream at the wedding breakfast, it seemed that she really was intending to cook pudding for breakfast. 'Sounds interesting,' he said neutrally. 'Shall I make coffee? And I could juice some oranges.'

'Thanks, that'd be great.'

Weird. If anyone had told him six months ago that he'd enjoy something as simple and domesticated as pottering around in a kitchen, while someone else cooked breakfast, he would've laughed. Then again, six months ago, he would already have been in his lab for a couple of hours, trying out ideas he'd woken up with.

How things changed.

Would he ever be able to do that again? In a few months' time, a year even, would things be back to normal? Would he be living his dream again, developing fragrances and feeling glad to be alive when he woke up, instead of feeling useless and a complete failure and desperately trying to hide the truth from everybody?

He pushed the thoughts aside and concentrated on making coffee, juicing oranges and laying the scrubbed pine table while she flipped a batch of pancakes; he set her at the head of the table and himself at the side, at right-angles to her. Companionable. 'Coffee's ready when you are,' he said, pouring it into two mugs and adding milk before setting the mugs next to the glasses of juice.

'Perfect timing. Sit down.' She put a bowl of whipped cream on the table, added another bowl with warm stewed apple and then slid a plate of pancakes between them. 'Help yourself.'

He was pretty sure he couldn't taste them in quite the same way that she did—with scent being such a large part of taste, he could barely make out the flavour of the cinnamon in the apple or the vanilla in the Chantilly cream—but the pancakes were light, fluffy and melted in his mouth, and the texture of the pancakes made a stunning combination with the grainy apple and the light-as-air cream. 'I admit, this is fantastic. You're very good at this,' he said.

'Thank you.' She inclined her head in acknowledgement of the compliment and gave another of those sunny smiles that sent a jolt of desire through him.

'I think you might be right about pudding for breakfast.' Guy helped himself to more. 'From now on, I'll always associate you with apples and vanilla.'

She raised an eyebrow. 'Isn't vanilla meant to be bland?'

Bland was the last word he'd use to describe her. 'No. It's sweet, but it's also amazingly sensual.'

'Why, thank you.'

He grinned. 'You have the cutest dimples. And when you blush like that…it makes me want to make you blush all over.'

'I'll take that as a promise,' she said. 'Later tonight.'

Why not now?

The question must have shown on his face, because she

explained, 'You probably have work to do, and I already have plans for today.'

'Oh?'

'I'm going exploring. You know, the list I made yesterday?'

'Uh-huh.'

Her eyes narrowed. 'What? You're thinking I'm a woman so I can't navigate?'

'I didn't say that. But you don't know the area.'

She folded her arms. 'There is such a thing as satnav.'

'True. But wouldn't it be easier for you if someone else was driving? Someone who does know the area, and can find nice places for lunch?'

'I don't spend my entire time having lunch, you know.'

He raised an eyebrow. 'That's not what you said yesterday.'

'I was cross with you.'

'And you're cross now.'

'Because I know what you're doing. You're trying to get me really cross with you, and then you're planning on having make-up sex with me.'

He laughed outright at that; he loved it when she was forthright. 'Are you calling me shallow?'

She rolled her eyes. 'You only have one X chromosome. *Of course* you're shallow.'

'You're wearing a skimpy bit of hot-pink silk and nothing else. What do you expect?' he fenced back.

'Well, hey, I'm just an airhead party girl.' She drawled it contemptuously, but he could see something in her eyes. He'd just hurt her. And he had no idea what he'd said.

'Amber?'

Her reply was a really, really bright smile. But he remembered what she'd said last night, and he knew that she was smiling to keep herself in control.

He took her hand and drew it to his lips. Kissed her palm, and folded her fingers over it. 'I can see I've just upset you, and I'm sorry for that. I don't know what I said but, believe me, I didn't mean to insult you. If you'd like me to drive you to the places you want to visit, I'm more than happy to do that.'

'Don't you have work to do?'

That was the rub. He did—he just wasn't physically able to do it, right now. At least, when he was with her, his attention was away from that. And her company might stop him brooding about the problem that seemed to be moving further and further away from a solution. 'I can take leave for a day.' He leaned over and stole a kiss. 'Thank you for breakfast, *mon ange*. I'm going to have a shower now— and if we're to have a hope of actually getting out of the château today, I need to have that shower on my own. See you by the front door in an hour?'

She blinked. 'Do you take that long to get ready?'

'No.' But Véra used to, so he had assumed that Amber would need the same amount of time.

'Give me five minutes to clear away here, and ten minutes to shower and change.'

'Seriously?' He was surprised—and impressed. And, because he'd just insulted her, he felt he owed her. 'Skip the clearing up. I'll help you when we get back—considering I ate half of what you made, the least I can do is half the cleaning,' he said.

'OK. Deal.' This time, Guy realised, her smile was genuine. Because it reached her eyes and it was a shade less glittery than her professional smile.

Though in fifteen minutes' time, when she met him at the front door, he looked at her feet and sighed. 'Amber, are you seriously expecting to walk anywhere in those shoes?' At least they weren't the pink ones, but they were very similar, this time in bright turquoise. They looked only suitable for a catwalk.

'I can walk in these. Well, unless you're intending to drag me up a mountain.'

'Which is exactly what I was going to do.' He sighed again. 'Don't you have any walking boots?'

'Living in London, I don't tend to go on long walks in the country at the weekend or what have you,' she said, 'so, no. I don't even *possess* a pair of walking boots.'

'Trainers?' he suggested hopefully.

She looked faintly disgusted. 'The only flat shoes I have are the ones for my dance class. And, apart from the fact that they're in London right now, they're ballet pumps so they wouldn't be any good on a mountain, either.'

Just when he thought she was different, she did something exactly like Véra would've done. Why couldn't he keep it in his head that she was from his ex's world? 'OK. We'll skip the mountain.'

'I'm not trying to be difficult,' she said. 'And I *can* walk in these. All day, if I have to.'

'Right.' He knew that was just bravado.

As if he'd spoken aloud, she lifted her chin. 'Want to bet on it? Because, if you do, I can tell you now that you're going to owe me a box of the best gianduja at the end of today.'

'And if I win?' he asked silkily.

She grinned. 'Then I'll eat it off you.'

There was nothing he could say to that. *Nothing.* Because the picture she'd just put in his head had rendered him temporarily speechless.

'What's the matter, Guy?' she taunted. 'All the blood from your brain just gone south?'

In answer, he pulled her into his arms and plastered her against him.

'Point taken,' she whispered shakily.

Oh, her runaway mouth. Was she ever going to learn? If she carried on like this, he'd despise her. And she really, really wanted to be different.

Knowing that she reminded him of his ex had shaken her. Amber wasn't the diva type, so why did he persist in thinking that about her? She was very aware that Guy disapproved of her world; he'd been there and hated it. But her world wasn't that bad—was it?

Being with him made her look at herself and reassess her life, and she wasn't entirely sure she liked what she saw. Her world was fun—but she had to admit that it was based on gossip and the latest hot trends. She spent her time chatting and shopping and lunching and partying. There was no depth to anything she did. And everything was done in a rush…including the affair she'd started with Guy.

But not everyone could change the world. Not everyone could find a cure for diseases, or be an inspiring teacher to a generation of children, or rescue people from halfway up a mountain. She wasn't special like that: she was simply Amber Wynne, party girl. And she was honest about who she was. She never hurt people intentionally. She made people smile and feel good. That wasn't a bad thing.

And she really had to stop obsessing about the differences between their lives. This was only temporary, so it didn't matter. Did it?

Guy had borrowed Xavier's car again, so clearly he'd meant it about mountains. Well, she'd walk up his wretched mountain in her pretty shoes, even if she had to pay for it with a week's worth of blisters. No way was she backing down.

He took her out to the north of the region, driving through a wild landscape of gorges and scrubby heathland. She noticed that he drove very steadily rather than speeding round the bends—and discovered why, when mountain goats skipped across the road in front of them, heedless of the traffic.

Though the scenery was stunning. And she loved the lake at Issarles, a huge deep crater filled with dark blue water and surrounded by meadows.

'It's prettier in the spring,' he said, 'when all the wild flowers are out. How are your feet?'

'They're fabulous, thank you.' Even if they had been hurting, she wouldn't have admitted it. Not to him. 'And this is pretty. So this is the volcanic part of France?'

'It is indeed—and I'm taking you to the longest lava flow in France, next.' He drove a little further into the Ardèche, through more of the wild, almost lunar landscape.

'*La cascade du Ray-Pic.*' She read the sign in the car park. 'That's the waterfall.'

'One of the most stunning you'll ever see,' he promised.

They walked through the woods and up some rough-hewn steps; Amber stumbled a couple of times, and was relieved when Guy took her hand.

'Are you going to admit now that your shoes are completely unsuitable?' he asked.

'Never in a million years.' But she didn't let his hand go. Not because she was worried about tripping, but because it was beautiful and romantic out here, and just for a little while she could pretend that they were really dating.

Which they weren't.

And wouldn't be, because they came from different

worlds and it just wouldn't work. This mad, crazy fling was just that—mad and crazy. And temporary.

She could hear the noise of water thundering down, and then suddenly there they were, watching the water streaming down over a striated volcanic rock face and landing in a clear turquoise pool at the bottom. 'That's beautiful,' she breathed.

'Here. Let me take a picture of you here,' he said, getting her to pose for him. And she persuaded him to stand with her so she could take a snap of them together on her mobile phone's camera.

'I had no idea that France could be so—well—wild,' she said.

'What did you think France was?'

She sighed. 'My experience of France—before this week—was Paris and St Tropez. Oh, and I did go skiing once at Val d'Isère.'

'Party girl,' he teased. 'I bet you skied once and spent the rest of the time drinking hot chocolate and admiring the mountain views.'

'Nothing wrong with that.' She laughed. 'Actually, I hated skiing. But the après-ski was fun.'

'Mmm, because even *you* couldn't ski in those shoes.'

'Why do you hate my shoes so much?' she asked.

'I don't. But this is the fourth different pair I've seen in three days. I'm just wondering how many more you have.'

She laughed. 'You really wouldn't want to know.'

'I would.'

'Tell you a secret.' She beckoned him closer, making him stoop so that she could whisper into his ear. 'I have a shoe room.'

He pulled back and stared at her. 'You're kidding me.'

'Nope. Actually, *What's Hot!* does this feature called

"What's in the closet?" and a couple of months ago they did one on my shoe room. The photo shoot was the most fun I've had all year. You can look it up online if you really want to see it.' She spread her hands. 'Hey, I did warn you that you wouldn't want to know.' And she couldn't quite read the expression on his face. Disapproval? He already thought she was shameless. Now he'd think she was a show-off, too. Time to salvage the situation and change the subject. 'Is it lunchtime, yet?'

He laughed. 'Hint taken. Let's go.'

They stopped in a little stone village, perching precariously on the side of a cliff, for lunch; the tiny bistro served fabulous food and Amber enjoyed every second of it. It was the lightest, most melting omelette she'd ever eaten, stuffed with ceps and served with some excellent rustic bread and slices of tomato scattered with basil and bursting with flavour. Guy chose home-cured sausages on a bed of lentils, and insisted on her trying it from his fork.

'Fantastic,' she said.

He coughed, and nodded at her plate. 'Fair's fair.'

'You want a taste?' She smiled, and made him reach for it.

When Guy allowed himself to forget that he was a nerdy scientist, she thought, he was fun to be with. Not to mention sexy as hell.

'Pudding?' he asked.

'There weren't any on the menu. I looked.'

'That's because they're on a separate menu,' he told her.

'Oh, what?' She sighed. 'That's not fair. I think I'm too full.'

'Shame. There's a chestnut pudding on the menu that's to die for.'

'Well, there are two ways we can do this. We can either

wait here for an hour until I have room for pudding—or you can order it and feed me a taste of yours.'

He raised an eyebrow. 'In other words, your feet are sore and you want a rest.'

'They are *not*.' She glared at him, outraged. 'Order the pudding. I can do this.'

The pudding turned out to be *pisadou*, layers of pastry filled with chestnut cream, vanilla seeds and *marrons glacés*.

'This is gorgeous. And I really like these.' She indicated one of the *marrons glacés*.

'Crystallised chestnuts. I have to admit, they're one of my weaknesses,' Guy said.

'Vice number what?'

'That'd be telling.' And his eyes had gone all sensual and hot; her pulse spiked in response. She made a mental note to look up recipes on the Internet for puddings that involved crystallised chestnuts, and make one for him. And they'd eat it in bed.

After lunch, he drove them south to the amazing gorges between Vallon Pont d'Arc and Saint Martin d'Ardèche. 'This is the French equivalent of the Grand Canyon,' he told her.

She could see exactly what he meant. There were incredibly steep drops, and she surreptitiously hung onto the car door handle. In places, the road went down to the water level, but most of the time they had stunning views of the river.

'In the summer, the viewpoints are heaving. But today we have the space to stop,' he said, and parked in a lay-by overlooking a particularly serpentine stretch of river so that she could take more photographs.

They ended up at the Pont d'Arc, a huge natural limestone

arch that stretched across the river. 'We could go shooting the rapids in a kayak, if you like,' Guy suggested.

'I'm up for it.'

He laughed. 'In your pretty shoes?'

'I can take them off. Just for the kayaking.'

'And you've done kayaking before?'

'Well—no,' she admitted. 'But it looks like fun.'

'Maybe another day. Let's chill out, instead,' he suggested.

They sat on the shore for a while, watching people canoeing and kayaking. On the way home, they stopped at another of the cliffside villages, and ate on the terrace of a bistro looking out at the sunset. Again, the food was amazing: a fabulous starter of langoustines with pink grapefruit and sesame seeds, then beef casserole with red wine and more of the chestnuts she was beginning to realise had a huge part on most menus, followed by delicate lavender ice cream and finally cheese and great coffee.

Guy held her hand across the table, and she realised just how easy it would be to fall for him. He was great company, charming and he was different from the men she usually dated—not one of her shallow, heartless liars. If she ever settled down, she'd want a man like this. Someone she knew she could rely on, who'd stop her being completely frivolous and yet who'd let her tease him into having fun. Someone who'd be her other half in all senses of the word.

Though she knew that man couldn't be Guy. He'd made it very clear that this was a fling, nothing more, and she didn't think he was the kind of man who changed his mind very easily.

Don't lose your heart to him, she reminded herself. Don't get involved.

Though a little part of her thought it might already be too late.

CHAPTER SEVEN

OVER the next week, Guy found himself getting closer to Amber. They'd fallen into a routine where she spent the morning reading on the terrace while he caught up with his work. She never interrupted him in his lab; she seemed to realise what a huge part of his life his work was. He knew she was curious, because she'd asked questions—sometimes very intrusive questions; but when he hadn't been forthcoming, she'd backed off. Maybe she knew he was deflecting her—she was certainly sharp enough to work that out—but he appreciated the fact that she'd give him the space he needed.

He usually took her out for lunch, and then they spent the afternoon visiting the tourist attractions. Amber still hadn't worn the same pair of shoes twice, much to his amusement; and he'd secretly looked up the feature on the *What's Hot!* website, curious to know whether she'd been teasing him or not.

She'd been telling the truth. And she'd looked gorgeous in the feature, all long legs and short skirts and glorious hair and kissable mouth. Although her smile had been bright, it hadn't been brittle. She'd clearly loved every second of the photo shoot, and the camera had loved her right back.

And yet here, in France, she'd enjoyed pottering about the château and taking over his kitchen. Which was the real Amber? The media darling or the domesticated angel? He still didn't have a clue. Though he recognised just how much he liked having her around. She made his world a brighter place, with her ready smile and sparkling eyes.

If it weren't for the fact that his sense of smell still hadn't come back and he'd started getting bad headaches—which he was pretty sure was caused by the stress of not being able to sort it out—he thought he'd almost start being happy again.

He checked his email. A pile of things that could wait; one he'd been looking forward to, the first draft of a design from Gina; and one he'd expected but hoped wouldn't materialise, another message from Philippe trying to persuade him to sell to the conglomerate. He sighed, and worked methodically through every single one of his business partner's arguments, chopping them into firewood. And then, just to sweeten the edge, he mentioned that he had the first draft of the design for the new perfume.

But before he pressed send, he opened Gina's file and studied it carefully. What would she have done with the brief for 'Angelique'?

To his delight, she'd captured the dual side of the fragrance: the sweetness of the vanilla base and the rose heart, and the edgy notes of pepper and myrrh. And what she'd come up with was a line drawing of an angel: very simple, with a hint of darkness around the wings. Not an over-pretty cherub, either—this was striking, sensual beauty, reminding him of a painting he'd fallen in love with once at an exhibition: Rossetti's 'Venus Verticordia.'

And then he wished he hadn't thought of that picture, because now he could imagine Amber in that pose. A coronet of golden butterflies round her glorious loose hair, surrounded by full-blown sensual roses and honeysuckle—and naked to the waist.

He really had to get his mind off sex.

And it was just sex, he told himself. He wasn't going to lose his heart to Amber, the way he had to Véra. He didn't want to get seriously involved with another party girl. Even if she did have a sweet, domesticated side that had surprised him.

He sent a quick email to Gina, thanking her for her work and giving her the go-ahead for the next stage; then sent the email to Philippe and logged off. And then he went in search of Amber.

They spent the afternoon wandering around the caves at Chauvet—Amber had mentioned that the cave paintings were the only bit she could remember from her History of Art course—and then headed back to the château. And in the evening Guy settled at the kitchen table, chatting to her as she pottered around the kitchen. Again, he found himself wondering which was the real Amber.

She dished up chicken wrapped in bacon and poached in apple juice, served with steamed green vegetables and a pile of fluffy couscous to soak up the gravy.

'This is fabulous,' he said.

She shrugged. 'I just like messing about in the kitchen. I actually found the recipe online,' she admitted with a smile.

Guy was even more impressed when she took pudding from the fridge. 'Crème brûlée and raspberries.'

'I made it this morning, when you were working.'

'It's my favourite.'

'Are you just saying that? Oh, wait—you said earlier that you loved vanilla.'

'Mmm. Though I also like the scent of amber.'

He realised what he'd said when she blushed to the roots of her hair.

'I'm sorry, *mon ange*, I didn't mean that the way it

sounded. I meant amber as in perfume amber. It's warm and rich and earthy, sensual and yet calming at the same time,' he explained.

'Sounds lovely.'

'It is. To make an amber base, I'd mix it with beeswax, then might add other notes, depending on whether I want it as a spicy or sweet base.'

'Which do you prefer?'

'For a woman's perfume, I like it mixed with vanilla,' he said. 'Which I'm ashamed to say is probably something to do with a lifelong love of *glaces*.'

She laughed. 'So you're an ice-cream fiend?'

'Have you not noticed the contents of my freezer?' he deadpanned.

'I imagine,' she said thoughtfully, 'that you're pretty sensitive to scent. Like a fashion designer seeing someone wearing a colour that doesn't suit them, or a good hairdresser seeing someone whose hairstyle is completely wrong for them—it must drive you crazy when someone's wearing the wrong perfume.'

Yes. It used to. And he'd been able to see people in terms of scent. But right now he couldn't trust his vision because his nose couldn't back it up.

Not wanting to explain all that, he gave a non-committal murmur.

'Oh, come on. You don't have to be polite. You can be honest with me.'

No, he couldn't. He couldn't be honest with anyone about the thing that was eating him from the inside.

She sighed. 'Is that why you're so moody?'

He blinked. 'What do you mean, moody?'

'One minute you're charming, the next you're unapproachable.'

'No, I'm not.'

'Guy, you are. You go all quiet and broody, and it's as if you've stuck a glass wall round yourself. Is this something to do with being a creative genius?'

'I'm not a creative genius.'

'Don't try to flannel me,' she said. 'Everyone says you're a genius. And you wouldn't be doing what you do if you weren't any good.'

That was the whole point. He might not be able to do it any more.

'OK, so that was maybe a bit too personal,' she said with a sigh. 'Either something is really bugging you—'

Oh, hell. Was it that obvious?

'—or you have to be the first person I've ever met who doesn't like talking about himself,' she finished.

Ha. Six months ago, if she'd asked him about his work, he would've talked her ears off. If only she knew. 'Some people don't like talking about themselves,' he said evasively. 'Let's talk about you instead.'

'You know me,' she said cheerfully. 'Shallow as a puddle. But, since you asked... Tell me.' She tipped her head on one side and smiled at him. 'Do I wear the right scent?'

It was a direct question, so he couldn't avoid it. But how could he answer? He could hardly tell her that he had no idea what she wore. 'I think something with amber and vanilla would suit you, maybe with a little bergamot to add some tartness to the mix—definitely warmth and sweetness.'

'You think I'm warm and sweet?' She sounded surprised, as if she hadn't expected that. 'I normally wear Chanel No 5. You know, like Marilyn Monroe—and my mum. So is that the wrong one for me?'

In his view, the 'classic' aldehyde scent would be too cool for her. But he wasn't exactly in a position where he could give her any decent advice. 'If you like the scent and it feels right to you, then it's the right one for you.' It was a completely anodyne answer, and he knew she deserved better. But, without explaining the problem with his nose, platitudes were all he could offer.

'But plenty of people wear clothes they like that don't suit them. They take advice from professionals.'

He didn't like where this was heading. Was she planning to ask him for advice? He couldn't give it to her, not without being able to smell. 'Perfume's more personal than clothes.'

'Is it? People have their colours done,' she mused. 'Having their scent done might be good, too.'

'It's not the same thing at all. People react differently to smells. It's all bound up with associations and memories. And how perfume smells on you depends on your skin—it doesn't smell the same on everyone.'

'Guy—'

He had to sidetrack her. Fast. 'Why don't you try making your own?'

'I thought it took ages to develop a perfume?' She frowned. 'I asked you about making a personal scent before.'

And he'd reacted badly. 'I know. But there's a business line I was thinking about developing, and you'd be the perfect guinea pig.'

'For what?'

'Come with me, and I'll show you.'

'What, you're actually taking me to the bat cave?' she teased.

'The bat cave?' he asked, mystified.

'Your lair. The secret laboratory, Dr.' She frowned. 'Are you Dr Lefèvre?'

'No. And my lab isn't secret.'

'It's certainly not public.'

'Amber—stop talking, will you?' Just to make the point, he kissed her. And by the time he'd stopped kissing her, she was beautifully pink…and mercifully quiet.

Until he took her into his lab.

'Wow. All those bottles,' she said, looking at his desk. 'I take it they're all different scents?'

'Yes. This is called a perfumer's organ,' he explained. 'Partly because it looks like one—' the bottles were set out in tiered rows on the desk, like the keys on an organ '—and partly because each bottle contains a perfume note. And mine is organised as top, middle and bottom notes.'

'The top note being what you smell first, the middle being the heart and the one you smell at the end of the day being the bottom?'

'Spot on,' he said with a smile.

'How do you know which fragrance goes with which?'

'Experience and experimenting,' he said. 'And, as I said before, everyone's taste is different. It's down to personal choice in the end.'

'It all looks really scientific.'

'Perfumery is an art. And you're creative—' at least, she was in the kitchen '—so let's see what you come up with.'

'It's not going to mess up your desk?'

'It's not going to mess up my desk,' he confirmed, touching her cheek with the backs of his fingers in reassurance. Again, she'd surprised him. He'd expected her to just sit down and enjoy being pampered without thinking about anything else. 'Sit down, *mon ange*. I'm going to give you some choices from the different fragrance families, and you're going to sniff them one by one and tell me whether you like it, loathe it, or you're not sure, and we'll build it up from there.'

'Supposing I pick the wrong ones?'

'You won't. As I said, it's a personal choice, so there's no right or wrong answer. This,' Guy said softly, 'is all about *you*.'

Amber was no stranger to pamper days. She had a regular slot for facials and massages. She'd been on pamper weekends with friends—and even for a whole week, once, when her mother was in the mood for a detox and wanted some company. If she was honest about it, Amber knew she'd spent her whole life being pampered.

But Guy was the only one who'd ever made her feel *special*. As if she mattered. As if she was really important. She wasn't used to that; in her world, she was just part of the crowd, another party girl.

Right now Guy was giving her his time. Full attention. And to have a hotshot parfumier helping her to make her signature scent…that was a rare treat. Something to be savoured.

She sat down at his desk, and he picked out a selection of the dark brown bottles from the racks in front of her and added some narrow strips of what looked like cardboard.

'What are these?' she asked, lifting up one of the strips.

'Smelling strips. They're made from perfumer's blotting paper—it means you'll be able to smell the scent but you won't accidentally get it on your hands, where it would start to blend with another fragrance,' he explained.

'And this is how you usually develop perfume?'

'If I want to test out some ideas, I'll put a couple of drops of each perfume base on the same blotter and let them blend. Obviously that's not precise enough for developing a formula, but it's a way of deciding whether I like the effect or not. It's kind of like musicians building up harmonies, trying different notes—except these are for your sense of smell, not your hearing.'

'I get that,' she said, smiling. 'So it's trial and error.'

'More or less. But I know before I start where I'm going. When I was training, I started with a brief—they'd tell me what kind of effect they wanted the fragrance to have, and I'd have to see if I could make the scent that created that effect. I suppose it's a bit like painting,' Guy said. 'Name a colour to an artist, and they'll be able to see it in their head. A trained perfumer sees the name of a fragrance and will be able to smell it in their mind—I know it sounds weird, but that's actually easier than smelling a fragrance and then trying to work out what the scent is. There are subtle differences.'

'That's fascinating,' Amber said, meaning it. And he clearly loved what he did, so why had he been so cagey about it before when she'd asked him? Something wasn't quite right, but she couldn't put her finger on it. If she asked him, she knew he'd deflect her—he'd done that several times already. What was he hiding?

'Before we start, you need to sniff this.' He handed her a small gold organza bag on the table. 'This is the equivalent of a sorbet at dinner, or bread at a wine-tasting.'

'You mean it's like cleansing my palate?' She was mystified. 'How on earth do you cleanse a sense of smell?'

'Just sniff it,' he said.

She did so, and recognised the scent immediately. 'Coffee?' she asked, surprised.

'It's an old parfumier's trick and it works every time.' He smiled at her. 'You'll need to refresh your sense of smell in between fragrances. I'm not going to tell you what any of the blends are called, because I don't want to influence you. Just remember that this is your perfume, so it's what *you* like that's important. And close your eyes when you breathe it in, to let you concentrate on the scent.'

'So what do we start with? The base?'

'No, the middle. These will give you an idea of the type of perfume you'll end up with, as they last for a few hours. Then we'll do the top notes, and finally the base notes to give it depth and solidarity.'

Going through each bottle in turn, he wrote a number on a smelling strip, dipped it into the bottle, then handed it to her to sniff.

'This one's gorgeous,' she said, picking out one of the top notes.

He smiled. 'Fitting. It's amber. One of my favourites, too.'

Heat coiled inside her at the expression on his face. Pure, unadulterated sensuality. 'Oh.' And she couldn't stop staring at his mouth.

He noticed—and stole a kiss. 'Keep going, *mon ange*,' he said.

The next one to go in her absolutely definite pile was one of the base notes. 'I love this. And I recognise it, too—it's vanilla.'

'Like your Chantilly cream. And the crème brûlée.'

'I'm going to end up with a pudding recipe, not perfume,' she warned.

'It's your perfume,' he reminded her. 'If you want to smell like pudding, *mon ange*, then that's fine. Gourmand perfumes are fairly popular.' He stooped and kissed the curve of her neck. 'Though it might make men want to taste you.' Just to labour his point, he nibbled her skin, making her arch back against him.

'Guy…' She shivered. 'I read somewhere that Chanel said you should put perfume where you want to be kissed.'

He laughed. 'Perfume smells better than it tastes. And it depends where you want to be kissed, *mon ange*.'

Her skin heated.

'I'd put you in a perfumed bath,' he said softly, 'so I could kiss you all over.'

'Now would be a good time,' she said, her voice cracking slightly.

'When we've finished.' His eyes held hers.

'What's the quickest you've ever made a perfume?'

'Patience, *mon ange*, is a virtue.'

'It's not one of mine.' She slid one of the straps of her top down her shoulder. 'And I thought you liked it when I wasn't virtuous.'

'Oh, I do.' He responded by sliding the other strap down. 'Now, concentrate.'

'What, when you just did that?'

'Uh-huh. If you want to be a scientist, *mon ange*, you have to ignore distractions.'

The teasing note in his voice warned her that he was planning more distractions. Very pleasurable ones. So she played along, took a sniff of coffee, then tried the next scent and grimaced. 'No. This one's horrible.'

'Oakmoss is meant to be mysterious.'

She shrugged. 'I suppose that makes me a little common then, not appreciating it.'

'No, it makes you honest. There's no point in wearing a scent you don't like. Moss can bring out notes in other scents, but if it doesn't work for you then don't add it in to your perfume, or you'll hate the final version.'

'Supposing I want to be mysterious,' she asked, 'instead of shallow as a puddle?'

'Trust me, *mon ange*, you're far from shallow.'

She hadn't been fishing for compliments, and she really hadn't expected him to say that. He hated her world and everything she stood for. How could he not think she was shallow?

'You have depth. That's in the vanilla,' he said softly. 'Sweet and sensual. Like you.'

'You really think I'm sweet?' He'd surprised her further, seeing things in her that nobody else had ever noticed. Making her look at herself from a different angle.

'And sensual. Let me show you something.' He switched on his laptop, flicked into the Internet and searched for a file. 'You know something about art or you wouldn't even have got a place at university. Do you know this picture?' he asked, showing her the screen.

'No, but from the style and the model, I'd guess it's a Rossetti.'

'*Absolument.*'

'And she's naked to the waist, Guy.' She folded her arms. 'That's a very Y-chromosome kind of thing.'

'She's as sexy as hell. She's dreaming of her lover.' He paused. 'And that sensual look in her eyes and on her mouth…that reminds me of you.'

'You see me like this?' She raised an eyebrow, but something in his eyes made her want to push him just that little bit further. 'Give me an armful of roses from your garden, and I'll pose for you.' She paused, and gestured towards the picture. 'Like that.'

'Really?'

'Really.'

His breath hissed. 'Stay there. Sniff the samples and keep sorting them into piles. I'll be back in a minute.'

He was going to cut an armful of his precious roses for her?

No, of course not. Apart from the fact that it was dusk, as soon as he walked outside the cool air would bring him back to his senses and he'd stomp back in and be ever so slightly grumpy with her for distracting him and tempting him to pick his roses.

In the meantime, she carried on sniffing the samples and putting them into piles, the way he'd shown her to do.

Though he'd left the laptop as it was. The more she looked at the painting, the more she could see why it affected Guy so much. The model was gorgeous; but, more than that, her eyes were dreamy. Guy was absolutely right in his assessment: Venus was thinking about sex. Remembering a lover's touch. And those memories, combined with the heady scent of rose and honeysuckle...

Guy burst back into the lab with an armful of roses, and her pulse rate spiked at the intense sensuality in his expression.

'I've taken off the thorns,' he said. 'So I'm calling your bluff.'

'Don't I need an apple and an arrow?'

He shrugged. 'Sorry. You'll just have to improvise.'

The heat in his eyes told her that he really wanted her to do this.

And she really wanted to do it, too. Pose for him. Make him weak at the knees. 'OK. Turn your back.'

He'd already seen her naked. But this was different, and all of a sudden she felt shy, near to losing her nerve. 'I'll tell you when you can look.'

He muttered something in French that she didn't catch, rolled his eyes and turned his back, leaving the roses on his desk.

Slowly, she peeled off her strappy top. Unhooked her bra. Folded them neatly and placed them over the back of her chair.

Oh, her big, impulsive mouth. It was going to get her in trouble again.

One of the roses was still a bud. She'd use that as the

arrow, and the bottle of vanilla as the apple. Improvise, he'd said—so she gathered the roses in her left arm and arranged them so they looked a bit like the hedge of honeysuckle. She flicked her hair forward over her left shoulder and back over her right, then transferred the perfume bottle to her left hand and held the rosebud in her right.

And then she thought about Guy, the way he'd made love to her that first time, and lowered her arm just enough to reveal her breasts over the edge of the roses.

'You can look, now,' she whispered.

Guy turned round, and colour slashed across his cheeks. He said something else she couldn't catch in French.

Worry flooded through her. Had she done it wrong?

'*Dieu*, Amber, do you have any idea how incredible you look, like that?' His voice was husky with desire. 'If I could paint…' He licked his lower lip.

'If you could paint?' she prompted.

'Then I'd paint you where I wanted to kiss you.' He took the rosebud from her and held it like a brush. 'Here.' He skimmed the edge of the petals along the curve of her neck. 'And here, where your pulse beats.' He touched the rose to where the blood throbbed. 'And here.' He drew it slowly down along her breastbone. 'And here.' He dusted it along the undercurve of her breast, making her shiver. 'And finally, here.' He teased the hardened tip of her nipple with the rose.

Oh, yes. She shivered. She really needed to feel his mouth on her.

'Guy,' she whispered.

And, the weird thing was, when Guy kissed her, he was sure he could smell roses on her skin. Right where he'd touched her with the rosebud. Of course he couldn't. He knew it wasn't physically possible. But his head was filled with roses as he took the flowers from her and dropped them on his desk.

She tipped her head back, and he kissed a path down the column of her throat. He touched the tip of his tongue to her pulse-point, and heard her give a breathy little sigh of pleasure. And then he followed the movements he'd made with the rose earlier. Between her breasts. Along the soft undercurves. And then finally closing his mouth over her nipple and sucking hard. Her hands were fisted in his hair, urging him on.

Time seemed to blur—and Guy was very, very glad that Amber was wearing a skirt rather than jeans, because he couldn't have waited long enough to take the rest of her clothes off. He needed her right here, right now. Just as he knew she needed him, because her hands were shaking as she undid the zip on his jeans.

'Condom?' she asked.

'In my wallet. Back pocket.' If there wasn't one there, he might just lose his mind.

She reached round to his back pocket, pausing to stroke the curve of his buttocks through the soft denim, then pulled out his wallet and handed it to him.

It was a matter of seconds for him to protect her. And then he was buried in her warm, sweet depths. She'd opened his shirt and his bare skin brushed against hers. Her arms were round his neck, her mouth was jammed over his and his head was full of scent. Vanilla, amber, roses. Things he'd always associate with her, from now on.

She held him tighter, and he pushed deeper into her, harder.

Their shared release, when it came, blew his mind.

And then he realised that they were both still wearing most of their clothes.

'I'm sorry, *mon ange*,' he said softly. 'That wasn't meant

to happen. Talk about no finesse.' He just hadn't been able to stop himself.

'Remind me never to go to an art gallery with you,' she said. 'I think we'd both get arrested.'

'I'd better, um, deal with things.'

She flushed. 'And I'd better get dressed.'

He kissed her. 'This was meant to be showing you how to make your own perfume blend.'

'If that's the kind of personal service you're intending for your clients, Monsieur Lefèvre, you're going to get yourself quite a reputation,' she said, giving him an arch look.

He smiled, and kissed her again. 'You drive me crazy. Do you know that?'

'It's pretty much mutual. I still can't believe you cut those roses for me. You're so precious about your roses.'

'You're worth it. The woman you are…' He stopped dead.

'What?' She frowned. 'What's wrong, Guy?'

'Nothing. That's it.' He could feel some of the clouds shifting away. 'My new perfume. "For the woman you are." That's the perfect strapline.'

'I like that,' she said, looking approving. 'But I'm not going to ask you for a preview, because I know the answer will be no.'

'It's no to everyone, right now. Don't take it personally.' He stole another kiss. 'But you definitely just inspired the strapline. And nobody's ever done that for me before.' He stroked her face. 'Back in a minute.'

When Guy returned, Amber was neatly dressed again, the roses were in a neat stack on his desk, and so were the piles of smelling strips—a small pile of definites, a similar-sized pile of definitely-nots and a larger pile of those she didn't mind.

'So are we going to make this perfume, then?' she asked.

'Sure.' He glanced at her pile of definites. 'You've got a good mix here—you've made a floriental. Amber at the top; vanilla, sandalwood and tonka bean at the base; and middle notes of rose, jasmine and orange blossom.' He fanned the sticks together and handed them to her. 'Wave them up and down in front of your nose, very quickly, and you should get the overall scent of the blend. What do you think?'

'It's nice.'

'But?'

'It feels as if there's something missing,' she said.

'You normally wear one with aldehyde top notes.' Or so she'd told him. One of the classics, though he hadn't been able to smell it on her. He sorted through her 'not sure' pile, fished out one of the sticks and slotted it into the fan. 'Try this.'

She did so, shook her head. 'No. That doesn't feel as if it fits. I don't know why, but it's wrong.'

'Interesting.' Just what he'd thought, then. The perfume she usually wore had the wrong notes. The vetiver would be right for her, and maybe the floral middle, but he would've added something sweeter to the mix, like the vanilla she'd chosen for herself. And something a little spicier. 'Let me try a couple of additions. And remember, this is your perfume, not mine. If you don't like the new notes or something still feels missing, tell me.'

She waved the fanned sticks in front of her nose, and felt her eyes widen in surprise. 'I have no idea what you just did, but that's *lovely*.'

'I added a little spice—cardamom and geranium.'

'It's perfect.' She smiled at him. 'It's got that mysterious note I wanted.'

He kissed the tip of her nose. 'Glad to oblige, *mon ange*. But you need to try it outside, away from any residual scents in here. Sniff the coffee, first, to clear your palate.'

She did so, and followed him outside, where she waved the fan of sticks in front of her nose again. 'Oh, wow. I *really* like that.' She tipped her head on one side and looked at him. 'What do you think?'

He spread his hands. 'Hey, it's your blend, your signature.'

'You helped.'

'Not much. Most of it was you,' he said. 'What are you going to call it?'

Her eyes sparkled with mischief. 'Number Three.'

'Very funny.' But he couldn't resist stealing a kiss.

'So is this the new business thing you were thinking about? Getting people to make their own perfume?'

He nodded. 'I thought I could work out maybe thirty or so blends that go well together and cover the main fragrance families. Then people could do what I've just done with you and make their own signature scent.'

'The ultimate pamper gift, designing your own fragrance? That's a fantastic idea,' she said. 'It's the kind of gift you can give people for special birthdays, Mother's Day and the like.'

'That's what I thought.' He took a pipette full of each of the scents she'd chosen, measured them into a glass bottle and mixed them together. 'Here you go. Number Three.'

'I know you don't like the name. What would you have called it?'

'Verticordia. After the painting.'

She took the bottle from him, and sniffed. 'Thank you. I'm already wearing perfume, so I can't put it on, can I?'

'It'd clash with the fragrance you use now. You'd have to wash yours off, first,' he said.

'Then I'll wear this tonight. After I've had a shower.' She inspected the bottle. 'Were you just going to give people a plain glass bottle, like this?'

'What, you want me to put this in a vintage bottle?'

'No, no, no—this is fine for me.' She flapped a hand. 'But, it's like I said before, little details make it. This bottle's perfectly functional but it's not pretty. It doesn't feel special enough to contain my own special perfume. I think you need to give people a choice of bottles, right from an inexpensive modern flask through to—well, yes, something antique and expensive, so you cater for everyone's needs. And that strapline you were talking about would work even better for this, because the scent's tailor-made for every woman.'

'That's a good thought.'

'And you need it in a box.' She was clearly on a roll, here. 'A plain one is fine, because you don't want to take the focus away from the perfume, but you need a ribbon to tie it. Something that matches a colour note in either the bottle or the tissue paper protecting the bottle.'

'Tissue paper?'

'Because, unless the bottles are all the same size and shape so you can use a custom-made box, you'll need something to protect the bottle inside the box.'

Guy looked at her, surprised. 'You seem to know a lot about packaging.'

'Because I'm one of these annoying people who spend hours wrapping presents,' she explained. 'I like adding all the flim-flam to make people feel special. The bows and the curled ribbons and maybe a sprinkling of confetti inside the wrapping. Details *matter*.'

'Like the candied rose-petals and the sparklers on your pudding.'

'Exactly.' She slid off the stool and kissed him lightly.

'Thank you for helping me make this, Guy. It's really special.'

And so, he was beginning to think, was she.

CHAPTER EIGHT

The following morning, Guy was making notes about the perfume launch when his email pinged.

Philippe.

And he wanted a meeting. Guy sighed inwardly. He had a feeling that this was going to end with him talking to his bank manager. Though if Philippe really wanted to leave the perfume house, it wasn't fair of him to keep his business partner hanging on. And email wasn't always reliable—especially when it came to making appointments. He picked up the phone and, when Philippe answered, said, 'It's Guy. I'm coming back to Grasse this afternoon. Do you want to meet at the perfume house?'

'Your office, two o'clock?' Philippe suggested.

'*D'accord*. See you then.' He replaced the receiver and went outside in search of Amber, who was reading a magazine and texting her friends at the same time. 'I need to go back to Grasse,' he said.

She raised an eyebrow. 'Problems?'

'No,' he lied.

She reached over and squeezed his hand. 'I wasn't fishing, but you look a bit tense.'

He shrugged. 'Just some things that need sorting out.'

'With your new perfume?' She stopped herself. 'Sorry,

I know I shouldn't ask. My mouth runs away with me sometimes.'

He stole a kiss. 'It's a beautiful mouth.'

'Thank you.' She paused. 'So I guess, if you're heading back to Grasse, this is goodbye, then.'

Ending things between them would be the sensible thing to do, he knew, especially as his life was about to get messy; it wouldn't be fair to drag her into this.

'Can I email you?' she asked.

He blinked. 'Email me?'

'Your idea about designing your own perfume—I've been thinking about that and I have some thoughts about it.'

'Why don't you tell me on the way to Grasse?' The words were out before he could stop them.

She looked surprised. 'You'd take me to Grasse with you?'

Tell her no. Tell her you've changed your mind. But his mouth wasn't listening. 'If you'd like to come with me.'

'I'd love to. I've never been to Grasse. The perfume capital of the world.'

Too late, now. He couldn't back out. Then again, part of him didn't want to. He wasn't quite ready to say goodbye to her.

Then her face turned serious. 'What about my hire car?'

He shrugged. 'We could take it back to the airport this morning. I'll follow you in my car, then we'll go on to Grasse together.'

'Offer accepted.' She smiled. 'So do I get to see the bat cave in Grasse, too?'

He laughed. 'I don't live in a bat cave. And the perfume house isn't a cave, either.' And he must really need his head examined.

* * *

It didn't take Amber long to pack. After she'd dropped off her hire car at the airport in Avignon, Guy drove them to Grasse.

'I've been thinking about this "design your own perfume" thing,' Amber said. 'It's a genius idea. I can see it working as a pamper party type thing—a lot of cosmetics parties have branched out into jewellery, and customised perfume's the obvious next step. We could even do a big launch party to generate more interest in the idea.'

'No.'

'Why not?' And then she thought about it. Of course. It was *obvious*: pride. 'Look, I know you're practically a master parfumier so you won't want to let anyone else make the blends, in case they don't come up to your standards, but if you're in charge of supplying the blends and you hold training days for, I don't know, beauty salon staff or the people who are going to do the pamper party—then that won't be a problem, will it?'

'I keep my launches low-key. Word of mouth. And it's only going to be available in the Grasse shop.'

'Guy, word of mouth is great, but how do you think people find out about things in the first place? They read about it, online or in magazines.'

'Which means intrusive journalists.' He gritted his teeth. 'No.'

'They're not *all* intrusive. Some of them can be a pain, I admit, but the beauty journos are all lovely. Allie's bound to have contacts from her days at the agency. And I have contacts, too. I could help you.'

'It's not how I do things,' Guy said. 'I thought you had some good ideas about the packaging, yesterday, and I'd be very happy to consider those. But absolutely no to the media.'

He really was being ridiculously stubborn about this,

and she couldn't for the life of him see why. 'Guy, what's your problem with the media?'

His problem with the media? Ha. He blew out a breath. 'You know I used to be married to Véra. The press hassled us a fair bit.'

'That goes with the territory, Guy—you have to be realistic about things. If you're a rising star in the business world and you marry a fashion princess, of course the papers are going to want to run the story about you. It's a fairy-tale romance and the public loves that sort of thing. It sells copies.'

'That wasn't the problem.'

'Then what was?'

'Fairy tales are just that—fairy tales. This was real life, and it got messy. And the paparazzi wanted front-row seats as our marriage disintegrated.'

She frowned. 'Didn't your publicist sort it out?'

'I didn't have a publicist.'

'Well, Véra must've had one. I mean—unless you're really good at PR yourself, if you're in the public eye you need someone to help you get the right spin on a story.'

That had never occurred to him before. 'You mean, she deflected the heat off her by setting them onto me instead?'

'I have no idea. I don't know Véra, and I don't know what happened between you because I don't tend to read the gossip pages anyway—well, not unless it's a story about one of my friends and I know I'm going to have to go round with cookies and tissues and sympathy that afternoon. I read features about clothes, make-up and shoes. And recipes, though if you tell anyone that,' she warned, 'I'll deny it and then I'll stick a fork in you where it really hurts.'

He couldn't help smiling at that. 'OK. I promise I won't rat you out to the press.'

She bit her lip. 'Guy, I wasn't prying.'

'I know you weren't.' He sighed. 'Look, if I tell you, then maybe you'll understand why I don't want the press involved and you might stop nagging me.' The memories stuck in his throat for a moment. 'Véra and I should never have got married in the first place. Or, at least, she should never have given up work.'

'She gave up work to be with you?'

'I think she had this idea that I would just go into the parfumerie for an hour or so, dabble around with a couple of essences and delegate everything else so I could go home to her.'

'She didn't know you very well, then,' Amber said. 'Or understand how your job works. But why didn't she do something like developing her own make-up in tandem with your perfume?'

'She wasn't interested.' He shrugged. 'Maybe if we'd lived in Paris, near her friends, it would've been OK. Or Nice, or even Cannes—somewhere that she'd be surrounded by people from her world. She hated being on her own.' He grimaced. 'She drove me crazy at work, ringing me every few minutes—and it was never anything important, just because she was bored and wanted my attention. "High-maintenance" doesn't even begin to describe her.'

'That's what you called me,' Amber said, sounding hurt.

'You're not that much like her. Well, not often,' he said.

'Thank you for the non-compliment,' she said drily.

'It wasn't all her fault. She wanted more attention than I could give her, and I didn't understand that, for her, everything was about being a celebrity and she missed her old life. I thought she was being princessy and demanding—and I did the worst thing possible. I shut myself in my lab for some peace and quiet. She thought I was ignoring her, when really I was just trying to avoid the fights.'

'And stop her throwing things at you?'

He must've looked surprised, because she said drily, 'I remember what you said when you got the knots out of my hair.'

'Yeah, she used to throw things. That's why I moved my perfume bottle collection to the shop. When it was in our house, it'd be the first thing she'd pick up and throw.' He rolled his eyes. 'I lost some of my best examples because of her temper.'

'Ouch,' Amber said. 'That's tough.'

'It got messier after that,' he said. 'It might've been different if she hadn't given up work to be with me, or if I hadn't been trying to get the perfume house up and running and spending too much time at work.' He shrugged. 'But then her agent called and asked her to go back to work. I thought it might help because, if we were both busy, then we'd appreciate our time together. Except she went on a shoot to New York, found a photographer who paid her more attention than I did and decided she wanted a divorce.'

'Hard on you—but probably for the best, since you were making each other unhappy.'

'Yes. I could cope with that.' He sighed. 'What I couldn't deal with was the media. They spotted her canoodling in New York with her photographer, and they refused to accept my statement that we were parting due to irreconcilable differences. They wanted the dirt behind the story. They wanted to know how I felt and they expected me to bleed on their front pages. I hated it, Amber. All the questions and the demands. It was relentless. At home, at the office, in my lab... They were everywhere. That's why I keep all my launches low-key, so I don't have to deal with that kind of thing again. It drives Philippe mad—my business partner thinks the way you do, that I should cosy up to them—but it's not the way I do things. And it's not negotiable. I don't want the press sniffing round.'

Especially because, if they started digging for dirt, the way they had when he and Véra had split up, they could find out that he'd been visiting doctors. They'd start adding up the clues and start speculating until one of them hit on the truth about his anosmia—and then all hell would be let loose. He had to keep the press at bay until he'd found the solution, dealt with it and no damage could be done to the perfume house. Not just for his own sake, but for the people who worked for him, who'd supported him through the tough times and didn't deserve to be let down so badly.

'Not all the press are bad, Guy,' Amber said softly. 'I'm sorry they gave you a hard time. But this wouldn't be that kind of story. This would be one for the features magazines. About how to make people feel special, the kind of one-off treat that would really put sparkle into someone's life. It's a feel-good, positive story.'

'No,' Guy said.

Talk about stubborn. The man was impossible. Surely he could see it would make good business sense? Though admittedly the journos probably would mention that he used to be married to Véra. She could see how that would rub a bit of salt in his wounds.

'Let's change the subject, as we're here,' Guy said. 'Welcome to the perfume capital of the world.'

The town was built on a hill, spreading down to what Amber guessed would be flower fields in the spring and summer; it was dominated by a church and a tower.

'I had no idea it would be so pretty here.'

'Apparently, it was Queen Victoria's favourite winter spot.'

'I can see why. Have you lived here for long?'

'For about seven years, now. Though I still get the same rush when I come home as I did when I first came here as a small child, when my mother brought me here to buy a birthday present for her aunt and took me to see all the old-fashioned lab equipment in the museum.'

'So you were the family's mad scientist even then?' she teased.

He laughed. '*Absolument*. Papa bought me a chemistry set for my birthday, one year, and my mother had kittens that I was going to blow up the château.' He parked in a narrow street. 'I'm afraid this is as near as we can get to my flat because the roads are too narrow for traffic in this part of town. This is the *vielle ville*, the old town. It's quiet and you can go for a stroll and just lose yourself in your thoughts without all the noise and fumes of traffic.'

He helped her out of the car, then took her cases from the back. 'This way.' He led her through winding streets that she could see were way too narrow for cars and were lined with ancient buildings—five-storey houses, painted in red-and-yellow ochre, with narrow doorways and tall, narrow windows with shutters painted in *eau de nil*. Everywhere she looked, there were old-fashioned wrought-iron lamps and hanging baskets filled with scarlet geraniums.

'We need bread and milk,' he said, stopping outside a delicatessen. 'Will you be OK if I leave you here with your cases?' At her nod, he said, 'I'll be two minutes, OK?'

While Amber waited for him, she took in her surroundings. Further ahead, the narrow street became a series of steps, and bistro tables were even perched on the steps outside what she presumed were cafés. Everywhere seemed fresh and vibrant and busy—and yet at the same time there was the slower pace of life she'd come to associate with Guy, people lingering over coffee and pastries and browsing through newspapers. She could see exactly why he loved it here. She could easily fall in love with this part of France herself—even more than she adored Paris.

He emerged from the deli with a baguette and a paper carrier bag. 'Would you mind carrying these for me?' he asked.

'It's OK. I can manage my own luggage,' she said.

'Absolutely not,' he said, and handed her his purchases before picking up her cases.

She could see it would be pointless to argue with him, so she followed him through one of the little narrow archways she'd noticed earlier. It opened up into a pretty square with a fountain and a tree in the middle.

'That's Grasse for you,' he said with a grin as she exclaimed in delight. 'Full of surprises. And this is where I live.' He gestured towards a town house that was painted a sunny yellow colour with grey shutters; the wrought-iron balconies were filled with pots of shrubs.

'This is all yours?' she asked.

'Only one floor of it,' he said. *'Bienvenue.'* He tapped in a code to let them through the front door, then strode up the stairs to the next floor.

Amber wasn't sure what she'd been expecting—something like the château, perhaps?—but his flat was a revelation. Most of it was open-plan: there was a small kitchen with cabinets painted china-blue and cream to one side, then a living room with a comfortable-looking cream leather sofa, a glass-topped table and two wrought-iron chairs set by one window and what looked like a seriously expensive sound system in the corner. The floor was polished wood, with a large Persian rug in shades of ruby, ochre and navy spread across the centre. There were voile curtains and cream drapes at the windows and the French doors, the walls were painted cream and hung with modern watercolours of what she guessed were places in Grasse. Along the mantelpiece, there were framed photographs of Xavier and two older people that looked enough like him and Guy to be their parents, and one of Guy laughing up at the camera with a chocolate Labrador sprawled all over him.

'Your dog?' she asked.

'Noisette,' he confirmed. 'I lost her just over three years ago, and then I moved to my flat.' He shrugged. 'It's just never been the right time to get another dog.'

She remembered the conversation they'd had, the night he'd let her take him out to dinner. He still missed his dog, and she caught the wistfulness in his voice.

'The bathroom's here, if you want to freshen up,' he said, gesturing to one of the two doors leading off the main room, 'and the bedroom's here. I'll make some coffee while you unpack, yes?'

'That'd be wonderful. Thank you.'

He took her cases through into the bedroom and set them on the bed. 'Help yourself to whatever space you need. There should be some spare hangers in the wardrobe.' He glanced at the lighter of her two cases. 'Though I'm afraid I don't quite run to a shoe room.'

'That's OK. The shoes can stay in their case.'

Guy's wardrobe was built-in, and the doors were painted the same colour as the walls. It was such a relaxing room, she thought: as light and airy as the living room, again with a wooden floor and cream walls, but here the curtains were navy blue and toned with the blue oriental rug next to the bed. The bed was king-sized, she noticed, with a wrought-iron headboard and soft-looking pillows and pure white bed-linen. There was a table next to the bed with a lamp, a clock and a book; she couldn't resist taking a look, wondering what he read for pleasure. Although it was in French, she was able to work out from the back cover that it was a biography of Marie Antoinette's parfumier. Guy had already admitted to being a workaholic, so she wasn't too surprised that his idea of a relaxing read was related to his work.

By the time she'd finished unpacking—and it felt strange to have her clothes hanging up next to his in the wardrobe, something she'd never done with any of her former partners—Guy had made coffee and set the table with bread, butter and cheese.

'Thank you,' she said as she sat opposite him. 'I love how you've decorated your flat. And those paintings are beautiful.'

'They're of Grasse,' he said. 'My neighbour downstairs is an artist. I bought them at her last exhibition.'

'I can see why. And they make me want to go out exploring, to see if I can find the places she painted,' she said.

'Maybe you can explore the town a bit this afternoon,' he said, 'while I'm in a meeting.'

She smiled. 'Oh, I have every intention of exploring. *Especially* the shoe shops.'

He eyed her in disbelief. 'You don't have enough shoes with you?'

'A girl can never have too many pairs of shoes,' she said airily.

'I submit.' He fished in his pocket and took a key off the keyring. 'I need to get going, so I'll give you my spare key.' He kissed her swiftly. 'I'll call you when I'm done at the office and I'll carry your new shoes home for you.'

'Excellent—you're well on the way to being trained,' she teased. 'I'll clear up here, first.'

'No. You're my guest.'

'And you have a meeting. I'll handle this.' She shooed him to the door.

He kissed her again. 'Thank you, for being so understanding.'

Amber cleared away their lunch things, then headed out to explore. She browsed round one of the museums, then spent a very satisfying half-hour in one of the shoe shops. And then she realised that the shop next door was GL Parfums; she couldn't resist going in for a look round. The shop was airy and bright, and the perfumes themselves were lovely, but what really caught her attention was the display of antique perfume bottles. They were so beautiful; why on earth had Véra smashed some of them in temper?

She bought some of Guy's posh shower gel for Sheryl, and then wandered through the old town again until she found a café in a pretty square. Despite the fact that it was October, it was still warm enough here to sit outside. Like an Indian summer day in London, she thought. She texted Sheryl to say that she was staying in France for a bit longer, this time in Grasse.

Two minutes later, her phone beeped. *With Guy? Just be careful and don't fall in love with him.*

She texted back, *'Course I won't.* But she knew even as she tapped the keys that she was lying: she was already doing that. For lots of reasons, and not just because the sex was good—she'd finally learned to tell the difference between lust and something deeper. She liked Guy's quick mind, and his ready smile, and the intensity in his gorgeous blue eyes whenever he looked at her. The way he argued with her, even—because it showed that he took her seriously and saw her as more than just a party girl. He thought that her ideas were valid and worth talking about. And he'd asked her to think about packaging for his 'design your own perfume' line.

Being with him made her feel different. He'd shown her a side of life she hadn't seen before—something with a slow pace, something with depth. And it was something she realised now that she wanted more of. That maybe in the past she'd rushed into things because she'd been looking for the place where she'd fit: and, now she'd stopped rushing, she'd found what she'd been looking for. Not where she'd expected to find it, either: with someone who was her complete opposite.

Although they'd said their affair was only temporary, maybe, she thought, if they took it slowly, this might develop into something more. Something with a future.

Could they make a go of it? It would mean compromise—probably more on her part than on his, she thought, because she'd be the one who'd have to move and change to fit in here. But he'd brought her here, to the more serious side of his life: the place where he lived and worked. And he'd let her into his lab at the château. To her, that suggested that he was letting her closer and taking his barriers down.

And maybe, just maybe, they had a chance.

She was still thinking about him when her phone rang.

'*Alors, mon ange*, I'm done. Where are you?'

'I'm sitting in a square, drinking coffee.' She glanced round quickly to find the street name, and couldn't spot it. 'Um, I'm not sure whereabouts exactly.' She named the café. 'And there's a florist's shop next door.'

'I know where you are. I'll come and meet you.' She could almost hear the smile in his voice: slightly amused, indulgent. No doubt most of the cafés in Grasse had a flower shop or a perfume shop nearby.

She'd just finished her coffee when he arrived. He stooped down to kiss her and sat down opposite her. Her heart skipped a beat as he smiled at her; she still couldn't quite believe that he was all hers, even though it was only for a little while.

He set some paper carrier bags on the empty chair between them. At her look of surprise, he said, 'This is dinner. I picked up a few things at the market on the way here.'

'I thought you didn't cook?'

'I'm not completely incompetent in a kitchen.' He shrugged. 'Though I admit I don't normally bother if I'm on my own. So how many million pairs of shoes do I have to carry?'

'Two carrier bags. Though I might have to go back tomorrow because I really should've bought this pretty scarlet pair…'

He groaned. 'You're a shoe-aholic.'

'What, you noticed?' she deadpanned.

When they returned to his flat, he started getting things out in the kitchen area. 'I'm going to make us a casserole. I'm sorry, there are a couple of little admin-type things I need to do while it's cooking, but feel free to take a shower or a bath or what have you.'

'I'll definitely take you up on that.' She blew out a breath. 'I can see why you're so fit, walking uphill all the time. My muscles are already protesting!'

He laughed. 'You get used to it, *mon ange*. Help yourself to whatever you need in the bathroom.'

She thoroughly enjoyed wallowing in a warm, deep bath filled with bubbles—especially as she could smell garlic and tomatoes and herbs, meaning that Guy was cooking something Provençal-style.

And then, a few minutes later, she frowned. She could smell burning. And it was getting stronger.

'Guy? Is everything OK?' she called.

When he didn't answer, she climbed out of the bath, wrapped a towel round herself—more to stop herself trailing water everywhere than for modesty's sake—and opened the bathroom door. She could see straight away what was happening: the heat was set too high and Guy's casserole had caught on the bottom of the pan.

Quickly, she grabbed a tea towel and used it as a makeshift oven glove, moving the pan onto a cold part of the hob. Guy was completely oblivious, working on a laptop on the table, with his back to the kitchen and headphones on. No wonder he hadn't heard her call out to him. But why on earth hadn't he smelled the burning? Even her father, the most focused man she'd ever met, wouldn't have been able to work through that.

She turned off the hob, then walked over to Guy and laid a hand on his shoulder.

He jumped, looked up at her and removed his headphones. 'Sorry, I didn't hear you call me. Is everything OK?'

'No.' She frowned. 'Guy, your fish is ruined.'

He blinked. 'How do you mean?'

'The ring was turned up too high and it caught on the bottom of the pan. Can't you smell it?'

He went white. 'Sorry. I got caught up in work and all my attention was focused elsewhere. I apologise for dragging you out of your bath—and for making dinner inedible. I'll take you out to eat tonight instead. There's a nice restaurant round the corner.'

'Guy, didn't you—?' she began.

'I'll deal with it,' he cut in, his tone making it very clear that he didn't want to discuss it. He'd gone moody on her again, putting up all his glass walls, and she had no idea why. Was this reminding him of some fight he'd had with Véra or something?

'Go back to your bath, if it hasn't got too cold.' He shooed her back to the bathroom.

Hell, hell, hell. This was worse even than he'd imagined it could be, Guy thought as he scraped the fish and the burned Provençal sauce into the bin. How could he not have smelled something so foul and so strong?

And it was obvious that Amber hadn't accepted his excuse that he'd been so focused on work that he'd blocked everything out.

Stupid.

Maybe he should tell her the truth.

But then she'd start to pity him, and he knew he couldn't handle that.

To his relief, she didn't mention it when she emerged from the bedroom, or on the way to the little restaurant in one of the squares near his flat. She kept the conversation light, telling him about where she'd visited in the town—and he knew he was being a lousy host, nodding and smiling at what he hoped were the right points but not offering much to the conversation. The knot of misery in his throat was too tight.

Even though the food was good, Guy could hardly swallow a thing, and ended up pushing his food around the plate.

'Are you all right?' Amber asked.

There was no judgement in her eyes. Only concern. This was the point where he knew he should open up. Tell her that he was far from being all right, and that his world was falling apart. He even opened his mouth to tell her.

But the words that came out weren't what he'd intended.

'I'm fine. It's just another headache.' That bit at least was true; the headache he'd had since that morning still hadn't shifted.

'Guy, if something's worrying you, you know you can talk to me and it won't go any further.' She curled her fingers round his.

'It's just a headache.' Guy forced himself to smile and be charming, and to his relief Amber responded. And when they went back to his flat, they sat on his balcony, sharing a glass of wine and looking out over the lights of the town in companionable silence.

Though he couldn't sleep. Even making love with Amber didn't help him lose himself completely: the worry was still there, at the back of his mind. In the end, he got up—quietly, so as not to disturb her—and closed the bedroom door behind him.

Maybe this time he'd find what he was looking for. Or maybe it was time he tried a specialist outside France. Someone who could help him right now, so he could put his life back together again.

CHAPTER NINE

WHEN Amber woke in the middle of the night, the bed was cold. Where was Guy? She could see a tiny crack of light around the edge of the door; clearly he was doing something in the living room. She climbed out of bed, pulled on her silky wrap, and opened the door. Guy was sitting on the sofa, hunched over his laptop, with his headphones on; he hadn't switched any of the lights on, so clearly the glow from the screen was what she'd seen.

What on earth was he doing on his laptop at this time of night? She couldn't see him as the type who'd mess about with social media, and he didn't strike her as the type who'd spend hours playing games online, either.

As she drew nearer she looked over his shoulder. The website was in French, and the title bar didn't help much: *cause et traitement d'anosmia.*

'Cause' and 'treatment' were easy enough to work out. But anosmia? It wasn't a word she knew.

'Guy?' she said, putting her hand on his shoulder.

He jumped, and nearly dropped his laptop. Hastily, he closed the page, then removed his headphones, closed the laptop and put it on his coffee table. 'Amber? What are you doing here?'

'I woke up and you weren't there. I saw the light, so I

came out to see what you were doing.' She frowned. 'Are you all right?'

'I'm fine.'

'You don't look it.' He looked haunted, and there were lines of strain around his eyes. And she was pretty sure it was to do with whatever he'd been looking at. 'What's anosmia?'

'Nothing. Go back to bed, *mon ange*.'

'I can go onto the Internet and put it through one of those translation websites,' she said, 'but it'd be quicker and easier for you to tell me.'

'I...' He sighed and shook his head. 'I don't want to discuss this. Go back to bed.'

'Guy, I know something's wrong. OK, so I don't know you that well, but over the last few days I've been finding it easier to read you—and right now I can tell that you're really tense.' She took his hand. 'You can talk to me.'

He said nothing.

She sighed. 'Guy, if this is something personal, it's not going any further than me. I promise you. And I always keep my promises.'

He still didn't say a word.

'All right. I'll look it up for myself.'

He closed his eyes. 'It's the inability to smell,' he said, his voice flat.

'But why are you looking at...?' she began—and then it hit her. And lots of things started adding up and making sense. Why he'd avoided her questions about his work. Why he hadn't smelled the fish burning. Why he'd put barriers up. 'You've lost your sense of smell?'

Bile rose in Guy's throat, thin and sour. The words echoed in his head: *you've lost your sense of smell. You've lost your sense of smell.* Slow and deep and monotonous, like a bell tolling. The death-knell of all his dreams.

He pulled his fingers away from hers and buried his face in his hands instead. 'Yes,' he muttered hoarsely. 'God help me, I can't smell anything.'

And then she was next to him on the sofa, wrapping her arms round him and holding him close.

'You need to talk about it, Guy,' she said. 'You can't keep something this big inside you. It'll destroy you.'

He already felt as if he were crumbling, but her arms were round him, shoring him up.

'Talk to me,' she said softly. 'I'm not going anywhere, and I'm not going to tell anyone what you say. This is between you and me. Just talk to me.'

He pulled her onto his lap. And at last, with her arms wrapped round him and his arms wrapped round her, he was able to let the words spill out. 'I had this virus. It must be three or four months ago, now.' He tried to sound casual about it, but he knew down to the minute when he'd first realised that something was wrong. 'I lost my sense of smell. I thought it was just the virus, but then I felt better and I still couldn't smell properly.' He damped down the shudder that racked through him.

'What did your doctor say?' she asked gently.

'He said I had to wait and see. So I bypassed him and went to a specialist. He said the same. And then I got a second opinion. I rang him for the test results, the day before the wedding.' He dragged in a breath. 'I'm sorry, that's part of why I was so rude to you that day.'

'That doesn't matter, now,' she said. 'What did he say?'

'He said that it might take up to three years. And also that I might never be able to smell properly again—there were no guarantees I'd get it all back. Which means my career would be finished.'

'Oh, Guy.' She held him close. 'Have you noticed any change for the better?'

'What do you think? I couldn't even smell the fish burning tonight.'

'But you were absorbed in your work.'

'Any normal person would've smelled it. You did.'

'I was lazing around in the bath. I've burned things before now because I was concentrating on something else.' She stroked his hair back from his forehead. 'Are the headaches you've been getting anything to do with it?'

He closed his eyes and rested his forehead against her shoulder. *Dieu*, he needed her warmth. And if only he could smell her scent. 'It's probably stress. Right now I'm panicking about what the hell I'm going to do if my sense of smell doesn't come back.'

'Have you talked to Xav about it?'

'How could I? The first couple of months, I thought it would all sort itself out. When it didn't... Well, September's harvest, Xav's busiest time of year. He didn't need the extra pressure of worrying about me. And then there was the wedding. It wouldn't have been fair of me to dump this on him and ruin his happiness.' He straightened up and blew out a breath. Enough of being weak and self-indulgent. 'I'm fine. I'll handle it.'

'You're not fine, Guy,' she said softly, stroking his face. 'Don't shut me out. Maybe you're putting yourself under so much pressure here that you're not giving yourself a chance to heal. Is there anyone who could take the heat off you, step into your shoes for a little bit? Your second-in-command at the perfume house, say, or your business partner or someone?'

'Definitely not my business partner.' The idea was so

unthinkable, he nearly laughed. 'Philippe's the last person I'd talk to about this.'

'Why?' She sounded confused. 'Surely he'd be the first?'

'At one time, maybe.' He sighed. 'The thing is, we've had an offer on the perfume house. From a large conglomerate. Our last perfume did quite well, and I suppose it brought us to the attention of the big players. And Philippe thinks we should accept the offer.'

'I take it you don't?'

'No. I like how we do things at GL Parfums. We're like a family. Everyone knows who everyone is, everyone looks out for everyone else. If you put some conglomerate in charge, things will change—it'll start getting faceless, full of paperwork and all about shaving down the costs instead of creating the best perfumes for our customers. We'll have to use the parent company's corporate suppliers because they'll be cheaper than the ones we use now—that, or drive the costs down so far that it'll push our normal suppliers out of business.' He shook his head in disgust. 'These are people I've known for years. People who gave me a chance when I started out, who've put in the hours and been loyal to me—how can I possibly betray them by selling out?'

'So don't sell,' she said. 'Buy Philippe's share of the business.'

'That's pretty much the decision I'd already come to. Buy Philippe's share and keep GL Parfums as it is—either talking the bank into giving me a loan, or finding another partner.' He grimaced. 'Though it'll be practically impossible to find an investor who doesn't want a say in how things are run. Philippe was brilliant until now, but he's bored and wants a new challenge. And it's not fair to make everyone at the perfume house face the same uncertainties with another partner, a couple of years down the line.'

'Why did you go into partnership with him in the first place?' she asked.

'Because I didn't want to wait until I'd made enough money to buy my premises and equipment outright. I was chasing a dream: having my own perfume house, developing scents that would be special to people—scents that were my own ideas, my own creations. There are people who think I wanted too much, too soon.' He shrugged. 'Maybe they were right. But at the time I thought I was doing the right thing. Philippe's the oldest brother of one of my university friends. He was on my wavelength, until now.' He blew out a breath. 'Well, it got a bit sticky six months in, when Véra decided to take me for every euro she could in the divorce settlement, but Xav bailed me out. We've done well enough for me to have paid him back last year.'

'So you can get a loan or find a new partner—that'll get the conglomerate off your back. So what's the problem?'

'People get bored with scents.'

She frowned, obviously not following. 'Chanel No 5's been going for years.'

'There are classics, yes—perfumes that have lasted for more than ten years—but the average lifespan of a new perfume is two years. The perfume market changes that quickly,' he explained. 'Basically, perfume doesn't stand still. You need to keep developing a scent, either introducing new ones or bringing a new twist to your classic lines. And, if I've lost my nose, I can't do that. I can't do my job.'

'Could you get someone to stand in for you until your sense of smell comes back?' she suggested.

'If I'm honest,' he said, 'I'm not sure I could handle that.

I'd hate going to work every day and knowing that it's not my vision or my creativity moving things forward. The new perfume's going to buy me a few months, but that's all.' He blew out a breath. 'I know I've got to find some kind of compromise, but right now I can't see what.'

Amber suddenly remembered how he'd described developing a new scent. 'You said it was like music. Well, Beethoven still composed when he was deaf, and think how fantastic his ninth symphony is. And you said that you smell perfume in your mind just from the name of the scent, so maybe you can still work?'

'The perfume starts off in my mind,' he said softly, 'but it's only once I've mixed it and sampled it that I know whether the formula needs tweaking or if the balance isn't right. So, no—I don't see how I can continue if my sense of smell doesn't come back.'

'Oh, Guy.' She hated seeing the bleakness in his face. 'It will come back. It has to.'

'That's what I've been telling myself.'

And he didn't believe a word of it. That much was obvious.

'OK, let's look at the really darkest side. If it does turn out that your sense of smell won't come back, then you can get someone in to help you so you can keep the perfume house going.'

'I know.' He dragged in a breath. 'But it won't be the same. It won't be my vision any more, my dream.'

'Yes, it will. Nobody can take away the fragrances you've already designed. Plus there's the "design your own perfume" stuff—I bet you already have a good idea which kind of blends you were going to offer. The person you get in to take over your old job can just fine-tune them for you. It'll still be *your* vision. And, after that…'

'That's what I'm most afraid of,' he said.

'Think laterally. Allie said you have an encyclopaedic memory, that you know about practically all the perfumes that were ever invented. You could be a perfume historian, the person the media comes to when it needs an expert quote.'

'Work for one of the museums, you mean?'

'Or set up your own museum. The important thing is, you don't have to shut yourself off from the world of perfume. You have all that knowledge. You could teach, maybe, write books about it. I know it wouldn't be the same as creating new fragrances, but you don't have to lose *everything*.'

'It just feels like it.'

Hating to see him so hurt, and not knowing how else to help, she cupped his face in her hands and brushed her mouth against his. Her lips moved against his, taking tiny nibbling kisses until he opened his mouth and let her deepen the kiss and take the lead.

When she broke the kiss, he was shaking.

'Guy, I don't know how to help you. I can't fix this for you, and I really wish I could.' She stroked his face. 'But I can do one thing for you—I can make you forget it, just for a little while, to give you a little headspace.' She kissed him again, and shifted on his lap so that she was straddling him; she could feel his erection pressing against her and rocked against him.

'Amber, I need to see you,' he said, his voice hoarse. He undid her wrap, letting her breasts spill into his hands. He teased her nipples with the pads of his thumbs until she tipped her head back, then took one nipple into his mouth and sucked, making her gasp.

'You're stunning, Amber, just stunning,' he breathed against her skin. 'And the way you make me feel…'

She held her breath. Did he feel the same way that she did? Was he going to say it?

But he let the sentence trail off, instead concentrating on kissing every inch of her breasts, lingering on the soft undersides until she arched against him, wanting more.

'Guy.' She dragged in a breath and slowly pushed his robe down off his shoulders. 'You're beautiful. Like a perfect sculpture.' She stroked his pectoral muscles, feeling the light dusting of hair tickle her fingertips. 'Except you're warm.' And all hers. Even if it was only for a little while.

He kissed her again, his mouth sweet and yearning. 'Take me to bed, Amber,' he invited.

She slid off his lap, took his hand and drew him to his feet, then led him back to his bedroom. She switched on the bedside light, then stood on tiptoe and kissed him hard. By the time she broke the kiss, his penis was iron-hard and he was quivering with need.

'Condom?' she asked.

'In the drawer.'

She found the foil packet, ripped it open and rolled the condom over his penis. 'All mine,' she said.

Guy was right where he wanted to be, lying back against soft downy pillows with Amber kneeling astride him, her beautiful curls all messy and her mouth looking as if she'd been thoroughly kissed. Somehow she managed to look wanton and regal all at the same time—and he wanted her. Badly. She was right: she could make him lose himself.

And he loved her for doing this. For being so generous with herself—so unlike his ex.

She wrapped her fingers round his shaft to position him where she wanted him, and eased slowly down over him.

'Oh, *Dieu*,' Guy said, completely lost, and her fingers tangled with his.

Pleasure built and built and built, leaving no room for any worries. All he could focus on was Amber: how good she felt wrapped around him, how much he loved the feel of her skin against his and how much he needed her.

And even though he knew he was being selfish, taking everything she offered, he lost himself within her; she was warm and sweet and comforting, pure balm to his soul. He pushed in deeper, wanting more, and she quickened her pace, rocking over him. At last he felt her body begin to tighten round his; as he fell into his own release he sat up and wrapped his arms round her, holding her tightly, as if he'd never let her go.

He never wanted to let her go—and how unfair was that? Right now, he had nothing to offer her except failure.

As if she felt him tense, she shifted and kissed him. 'Don't start thinking again, Guy,' she whispered. 'Just be.'

Oh, he could fall in love with this woman.

Could?

No, it was too late for that. He'd already fallen in love with her. With her sunny smile and her soulful eyes and the sheer unabashed pleasure she took in things. So what if she was a party girl, a media darling like his ex? Somehow that had stopped mattering. She was warm and sweet and like sunshine on a frosty day. And she made his world a better place. Especially right now, when everything felt so dark and constricting that he could hardly breathe.

Gently, he moved her off him and kissed her swiftly.

Afterwards, he climbed back into bed with her and settled with her in his arms, his body curved spoon-style round hers. As he heard her breathing grow deep and regular he brushed his mouth against her shoulder. '*Je t'aime*, Amber,' he whispered. Words it wouldn't be fair to say to her when she was awake, but words he needed to say to her. *'Je t'aime.'*

If only things could be different.

CHAPTER TEN

AMBER woke before Guy, the next morning. In sleep, he looked relaxed, with none of the strain or wariness in his face.

If only I could fix your world for you, she thought. But I can't. I know how important your work is to you. Nothing will be able to take its place and I won't be enough to stop you missing it, no matter how hard I try. I love you—not just because you look gorgeous and you make my knees go weak, but because you're different. You're not like my losers and liars. You're honest and you're clever and you're serious; but you're also witty and fun to be with, and you make me see the world in a different way.

But I also know that my love isn't going to be enough for you. You need more. You need to be able to create your fragrances. Without that, you won't feel that you're yourself: and I don't know how to make you see that yes, your work's important, but there's also more to you than that.

Quietly, she slid out of bed, borrowed his bathrobe— it was too big for her and she needed to wrap the belt round herself twice, but it was warm and comforting and it smelled of him—and went to make them both some coffee.

He was awake when she brought the mugs through. She kissed him gently. 'How's your head?'

'I'm getting used to waking up with a headache,' he said. 'It's OK.'

She almost suggested that he took the day off; but then, the way things were going, he was likely to have more days than he wanted away from his work in the future. Better that he enjoyed whatever time he could at the perfume house. She climbed back into bed with him. 'Anything I can do?'

He kissed her. 'No, but you're lovely—do you know that? You make my world a brighter place.'

She laughed, but his words warmed her deep inside. He made her world a brighter place, too. And, coming from a private man like Guy, it was practically a declaration of his feelings. 'Very smooth, Monsieur Lefèvre. Thank you for the compliment.'

'What are you going to do today?' he asked.

'I assume you're going to be working, so I might wander round town.'

'I do have a pile of meetings,' he admitted. 'And I need to work on the new perfume. Gina's sent me the design, and it's good.'

'Of course it is. She's brilliant. And your new perfume is going to knock everyone's socks off.' She paused. 'Guy, do you have a model in mind?'

He raised an eyebrow. 'Are you offering?'

'No. But I do know someone gorgeous who never does ads for beauty products, even though people are always asking her. And I know she'd make an exception for you, if I asked her.' She lifted her chin. 'My mum. That'd get you tons of publicity—the fact that Libby Wynne's modelling for you.'

'Trying to fix things for me, *mon ange*?'

'In my airhead party-girl way.'

'There's nothing airhead about you, and you know it,' Guy said. He glanced at the clock. 'And I'm going to be late if I don't get a move on. Thank you for the offer—I'll think about it, if you don't mind?'

'Of course.' He was being nice about it, but she knew she'd been pushy. It was just that she so badly wanted to do something to help. To make his world right again.

Sheryl, her best friend, was engaged to a doctor. Hugh worked with children rather than adults, but he was bound to know a specialist in his hospital who dealt with nose problems and might have some suggestions that Guy's doctors hadn't already thought of. After she'd kissed Guy goodbye and waved him off to work, she sent Sheryl a text, explaining the situation and asking her if Hugh could give her any advice. *Obviously this has to stay confidential*, she added—even though she knew she didn't really have to say it. Sheryl was her best friend and she knew the hassles Amber had had with *Celebrity Life*.

She spent the rest of the morning reading up about anosmia on the Internet, and what she read made her heart ache. Guy must be going crazy. Waiting would definitely drive her nuts, and her sense of smell wasn't that important; her career didn't depend on it, the way Guy's did. But she was shocked to discover that loss of smell also caused loss of taste. If she was in Guy's position and knew that she'd never again be able to taste a ripe, freshly picked English strawberry still warm from the sun, or the sharpness of blue cheese on fresh bread, she'd be so miserable.

Please, she begged silently, let Hugh be able to come up with something new. Something that could fix things for Guy.

In the afternoon, Amber explored more of Grasse, wandering round tiny churches and gardens that would no doubt be even prettier in the spring. She could really understand why Guy loved it here. She was falling for the place herself.

When Guy came home, that evening, he looked tired, so she refused his offer of dinner out. 'Put your feet up. I wasn't sure what we were doing tonight so I picked up some fresh pasta, bread and salad at the market, in case you wanted to eat in. It's not as if it'll take more than five minutes to cook.' She didn't want to admit just how much she was enjoying pottering round and being domestic. The people in her usual social set would laugh at her, with the exception of Sheryl; and, although she knew that Guy wasn't like them, she didn't want him to feel pressured. As if she had *expectations*.

'It's really sweet of you,' Guy said, 'but I'm not expecting you to wait on me.'

'I know. If you did, I wouldn't have offered.'

He laughed. 'That's contrary.'

'No. It's because you don't take me for granted that I'm happy to do it.'

'Then thank you, *mon ange*. Pasta, bread and salad would be very nice.'

Though she could still see the strain in his face after they'd had dinner. 'Another headache?' she asked gently.

'Yes. I'll take some paracetamol and it'll be fine.'

'Come and sit with me,' she said. 'Lie with your head in my lap, and I'll massage your scalp. One of my friends taught me how to do Indian head massage, and it's brilliant.'

'Now there's an offer I won't refuse.' He took a headache tablet, then came to sprawl on the sofa with her. He closed his eyes as she slid her fingers into his hair and started to massage his scalp and temples. 'That feels good, *chérie*. Thank you.'

'Pleasure.' She stroked the hair away from his forehead. 'So how was your day?'

'OK. I've given Gina the go-ahead. And I had an appointment at the bank to discuss buying Philippe's share of the perfume house.'

Which was one of the biggest weights on him right now, she knew. And she'd been thinking about how she might be able to help. 'Guy, if you need a business partner, I'm sure my d—'

He reached up to press his fingertip gently against her mouth, stopping her saying any more. 'Thank you for the offer, *mon ange*, but I'm OK. Really. I can sort this for myself. Things might be a bit tight for a while, but the deal's on the table. They're going to tell me their decision first thing tomorrow morning. I've worked out a business plan, and I'm pretty sure they're going to say yes.'

'Of course they will. You're fantastic at what you do and you're just about to launch a new perfume that's going to be the height of cool. You're an excellent risk.'

Though they both knew what she wasn't saying.

He was an excellent risk, provided his sense of smell came back.

And, if it didn't…

Then his future could be very tough indeed.

'Will you ring me when you hear?' she asked, the next morning as he opened the front door to leave.

'Of course, *chérie*.' He kissed her goodbye. 'Wish me luck.'

'Break a leg,' she said, trying to sound bright and cheerful, for his sake.

But she was fidgety all morning, worrying about Guy. The only thing she could think of to keep herself occupied was to do some baking. Luckily there was a grocer's just round the corner where she could buy the ingredients she needed—along with a vanilla pod and chocolate.

Keeping her hands busy helped to calm her down; the scent of vanilla cupcakes and choc-chip cookies helped even more, but it also made her realise just how difficult it was for Guy. Losing a sense, for her, would make her life flat. For him, it was his whole life. The thing that made him himself. If his sense of smell didn't come back, he'd be in hell.

She was halfway through getting the last batch of cookies out of the oven when her phone began to ring and when she saw it was Guy, she almost dropped the tray. She managed to shove it on top of the hob in time, then grabbed her phone—just as the call went through to voicemail.

'No-o-o!' Voicemail wasn't good enough. She needed to talk to him.

She gave it fifteen seconds for him to leave a message and end the call—which felt more like fifteen minutes, the second hand on the clock dragged round so slowly—and rang him. Engaged. She ended the call, pressed redial and kept doing it until at last his phone rang.

'Guy? Sorry, I haven't checked voicemail but I was getting cookies out of the oven when you rang. What happened?'

'You've been baking?'

'It was that or chew my nails off. What did they say?'

'You know how banks are.'

'Guy, I swear, I'm going to smack you over the head with the cookie tray when I see you if you don't tell me *right now.*'

He laughed. 'They said yes, *mon ange.*'

She whooped. 'Brilliant.'

'So I'm playing hooky and taking you to lunch. In fact, we're going to be out all afternoon.'

'Is this a good idea? Don't you have work to do?'

'It can wait. Right now I want to celebrate. With you.'

He was home within fifteen minutes. And he ate three cookies in quick succession after walking through the front door.

'You didn't taste a single one of those, did you?' she asked wryly.

He spread his hands. 'Hey. I had to check.' He gave her the most disarming smile. 'The texture was good, though,' he added.

'Thank you. I think.'

He kissed her swiftly. 'I'm going to change. You're fine as you are—you just need shoes.'

'Funny you should say that. I bought that scarlet pair, yesterday.'

He laughed. 'Now why doesn't that surprise me?'

They walked down the hill to where he'd parked his car, and he drove them south, towards the sea.

'We're going to the beach?' she asked.

'I was actually going to take you to Le Suquet, the old part of Cannes, but if you really want to go and do the touristy thing and walk along La Croisette and put your hand on top of a celebrity handprint, or go shopping in designer boutiques, we can do that.'

'No, that's fine. Though if there's a shoe shop in Le Suquet, I might be forced to go in.'

He laughed. 'Lunch, first, I think.'

Le Suquet turned out to be really pretty, with fantastic views of the old port and the bay. And, after a leisurely lunch at a tiny bistro, Amber enjoyed wandering through the narrow streets with Guy, their arms wrapped round each other. She took pictures over the bay in the late afternoon, when the sun made the water look incredibly enticing. 'This has to be one of the nicest days I've ever spent,' she said.

'Me, too,' he said.

Their eyes met, and for a moment Amber couldn't breathe. Was he going to say it…?

But he simply tucked an errant curl behind her ear. '*Mon ange*,' he said softly.

Angel. It was the loveliest, sweetest endearment. But she so badly wanted to hear the three little words that should go with it.

She could see he was looking at her mouth, so she tipped her head back in offering. He smiled and cupped her face in his hands. 'You're adorable.'

So are you, Amber thought as he kissed her. And I love you. And I want you to love me back.

But now wasn't the time to go all princessy and demanding on him, the way his ex had. He had more than enough to deal with. The best thing she could do was hold his hand, telling him without words that she'd be there for him. And maybe, when this was all sorted out, maybe she could be brave and say it first. And maybe, just maybe, he'd say it back.

Even though Guy hadn't made a declaration, Amber thought he was different with her after that. It felt as if they were closer, and there was an extra depth and sweetness when he smiled at her. And although he hadn't actually asked her to move to France to be with him, he also hadn't suggested that she should go back to England. Which gave her hope.

On the Wednesday morning, she was having breakfast with Guy when her phone rang. Amber checked the display.

She smiled at Guy. 'Do you mind? It's Sheryl.'

'It's fine, *mon ange*. It gives me a chance to catch up with the business news.'

While he immersed himself in the newspaper, Amber went to sprawl on the sofa and chat to Sheryl. When she ended the conversation, she went back to the table and swallowed a cup of coffee in silence.

'What's the matter?' Guy asked.

'I just spoke to Hugh—Sheryl's fiancé. He's a doctor,' Amber said. She dragged in a breath. 'I hope you don't mind, but I asked him about your anosmia.'

'You did what?' Guy's eyes narrowed.

'He's a children's doctor—but most of his friends are doctors, too. And he's bound by confidentiality,' she added hastily, guessing what Guy's real issue would be, 'so he's not going to be talking to anyone. Neither will Sheryl. I'd trust her with my life. And I didn't say it was about you. I said I was asking about someone…someone I knew.' And they both knew that Guy had become more than just an acquaintance.

Guy said nothing, so she ploughed on. 'He's been off duty for a few days, and then the person he knew who works in that area was off duty—but they went out for a drink together last night. Apparently, the most common cause of anosmia is polyps.'

'I know that and I've already had a camera up my nose,' Guy said. 'If there were polyps, surely my specialist would've seen them already?'

'I don't know. I'm not a medic,' Amber said. 'But Hugh said if you're getting headaches, it might be worth going back again and asking them to repeat the test.'

'The headaches are from stress,' Guy said. 'Sure, I can ask them to do the camera thing again, but I know what they're going to say. The same as they've been telling me all along. That I have to wait—' his face tightened with frustration '—and see.'

'Thank you for shooting the messenger,' Amber said drily.

He slid his arms round her and held her close. 'I'm sorry, *mon ange*. I know you were trying to help, and I appreciate that. I shouldn't take out my frustrations on you.'

'I just wish I could wave a magic wand,' she said.

'So do I. But it's not going to happen.' He sighed. 'I can't see that anything will have changed in a month, but I'll make another appointment with my specialist. And thank you for trying.'

'Trying?' Her mouth twisted. 'I didn't exactly do anything useful, did I? You already knew what I told you.'

'You cared enough to talk to someone for me who might've been able to help. And you've been there for me. You've helped me see that if the worst does happen, it's not the end of the world because I can still be involved in the business—just in a different role. You've helped me come to terms with that, which hasn't been easy at all.'

She'd really done that for him?

He stole a kiss. 'And you haven't given me a hard time for getting up at stupid o'clock because I can't sleep, then coming back to bed freezing cold and warming myself up on you.'

'That,' she said with a grin, 'is because you wake me up so nicely, Monsieur Lefèvre.'

'Mmm. And if I didn't have a meeting with Philippe this morning, I'd carry you back to bed right now.' He kissed her again. 'But I'd better go. What are you up to, today?'

'I thought about catching the bus into Nice and seeing what their shoe shops are like.'

He laughed. 'I should've guessed. Don't bother with the bus. Take my car.' He handed her the keys.

'Won't you need it?'

'No. Go and find some nice shoes.' His eyes were full of laughter. 'And some matching underwear might be nice. I'll take you out to dinner tonight, and you can model them for me afterwards.'

'And then you can take them off me.'

'You're the perfect woman, *mon ange*. You can even read my mind,' Guy teased.

She laughed. 'It's not that difficult, Guy. You have a Y chromosome.'

He stole a last kiss. 'I'd better be going.' He paused by the door. 'And, just so you know—it isn't just sex. You and me, I mean.'

Was that his way of telling her that he loved her? That he felt the same way about her as she did about him? Amber wanted to run after him and ask him what he meant, ask him to explain in words of one syllable. Preferably three words.

Did he love her?

Tonight, maybe, he'd tell her.

And that, she thought, would be a moment worth all of her favourite shoe purchases rolled into one. The best moment of her life.

CHAPTER ELEVEN

THOUGH things didn't go quite according to plan. Guy came back from the perfume house in a dark mood, and he was quiet all through dinner. Even modelling her new shoes and underwear for him didn't lighten his mood; in the end, Amber just held him close. 'Guy. It's going to work out. It *has* to.'

Though he clearly didn't believe her. And when she woke in the night, finding his side of the bed empty, she knew exactly where he'd be. Hunched over his laptop, desperately trying to find someone or something that could help him. She pulled on her wrap and padded out to the living room.

He looked up from the laptop. 'I didn't mean to disturb you.'

'Come back to bed, Guy. You'll wear yourself out.'

He said nothing, but to her relief he switched off his laptop and let her take him back to bed. Though it was a long, long time before she could get back to sleep again.

When Guy's mobile shrilled, the next morning, he groaned, rolled over and answered it. 'Lefèvre.'

Amber could hear the person on the other end shouting, though she couldn't make out the exact words. And then Guy jackknifed up to a sitting position. 'What? Uh.' He sighed. 'Yes, it's true. No, Philippe, I wasn't—look, this is pointless. Meet me in the office in half an hour and I'll explain properly.' He ended the call and said something very savage that Amber guessed was a tirade of expletives.

'Guy? What's wrong?' she asked.

'*Dieu*, I really should've seen this coming. What an idiot I am.' He shook his head, looking disgusted. 'So much for trusting your friend with your life. She wasn't exactly careful with mine.'

'What?' What was he talking about? She didn't understand. Frowning, Amber sat up.

'That was Philippe. He's just been contacted by a journalist wanting to know if the story's true—that we're selling GL Parfums because I've lost my nose.'

'What? But—but—' Ice trickled down her spine. How on earth could the press know anything about Guy's problem with his sense of smell? She digested what he'd said. He thought *Sheryl* had told them? She shook her head. 'No, it couldn't possibly have been Sheryl. She'd never do anything like that. She's my best friend. I've known her since I was twelve—for more than half my life,' Amber said. 'It *couldn't* have been her. Or Hugh. He's a doctor.'

'What difference does that make?'

'I know them—*both* of them—and neither of them would deliberately hurt you. Or me.' She shook her head. 'No way would they talk to a journalist.' But if the news had leaked out, it could cause huge disruption. And then a really nasty thought hit her. It might even destroy Guy's business.

Guy had already powered up his laptop and was checking the news sites. '*Merde*. It's everywhere.'

'Maybe it's the conglomerate, trying to drive the price down.'

'Then why didn't they try that months ago? Why now?

Funny how it happened just after your so-called friend discussed it with a colleague.'

'Sheryl and Hugh would never, ever break a confidence like that,' she repeated. To prove it, she grabbed her phone and speed-dialled Sheryl.

The phone was ringing when Guy tapped her on the shoulder and pointed out another story. French Parfumier Seeks English Help.

Oh, no. And it was all about how he'd used an intermediary to get advice from an English doctor, after French doctors couldn't help him. So the leak had to be from Hugh or Sheryl. But how? She couldn't imagine either of them betraying her like that. She just *couldn't.*

'Bambi?' Sheryl was crying as she answered the phone. 'Oh, Bambi, I'm so sorry. This is such a mess.'

Amber realised that her friend must have heard the stories spreading through the press. 'I know, we've had calls already.'

'I didn't say a word to anyone—only to Hugh, like you asked me to.' Sheryl's breath hitched. 'We had a huge fight about it this morning because I accused him of selling you out. He's so angry with me. I think he's going to move out.'

'Oh, honey—hang in there, he'll calm down.'

But whether Guy would ever forgive her... She couldn't see that happening. The way things were going, it was highly likely that he'd lose the perfume house. All his dreams, everything he'd worked so hard for. *Because of her.* She could see that he was on the phone again, and he was looking grim. Which left her torn. She needed to support her best friend—but, right now, she had a feeling that Guy needed her more. 'I'll call you later, OK? Don't worry, honey. It'll work out.'

And she'd do whatever it took to fix this.

'That was the bank.' Guy put down the receiver very coolly and calmly, and it was somehow worse than if he'd slammed it down in anger, because it meant he'd gone past the point of rage into pure coldness. 'They're scrapping the deal.'

Amber caught her breath in shock. 'But they can't.'

'Oh, but they can, *mon ange*,' he said bitterly. 'Because I didn't give them all the pertinent information in the business plan. I didn't tell them that I couldn't smell any more, so I can't do my job. Which makes me a complete no-no in terms of risk—and I'm the one who breached the contract terms, so I can't do a thing about it.'

'It wasn't Sheryl who leaked the story,' she said to Guy. 'And I don't think it was Hugh, either.'

'Then who was it? Mr Invisible?' He raked a hand through his hair. 'Oh, *Dieu*. I need to go to the perfume house. I need to call everyone in, to reassure them that the perfume house isn't going under, they're not going to lose their jobs and we're going to get through this. Somehow. And then I need a meeting with Philippe to see if I can buy some time to find another source of finance.'

Guilt flooded through her. The story wasn't just going to affect Guy. It was going to affect everyone who worked for him, too. She stared at him, stricken. She'd always thought the gossip magazines irritating but basically harmless; but now she was witnessing firsthand what they could do to people's lives.

Destroy them.

If he needed another source of finance, she could definitely do something about that. Either ask her father for help, or talk to the trustees to see if they'd release money from the fund she lived off. 'Guy—'

'Save it. I don't want to hear,' he said, and headed for the shower.

He was ready to go in less than ten minutes. 'I don't know when I'll be back,' he said, and walked out.

And although she could understand why he didn't kiss her goodbye, it hurt. Hurt like hell. Surely he must know that she would never have betrayed him like that? She would never have done anything to hurt him. The world felt as if it were crumbling beneath her feet. This couldn't be happening. It just couldn't.

But the story was all over the Internet. No doubt it would be in the local press, too. And, to her horror, she discovered that *Celebrity Life* was even running a poll on how long it would take her to dump Guy now that he was losing his business. What? She'd had no idea they even knew that she was seeing him. And now this... Did people *really* think she was so shallow that she'd desert her man the second that things got tough? That hurt so much that, for a moment, she couldn't breathe.

Guy's landline started ringing. Should she answer it, or would it be the press? She let it go through to the answering machine, and heard a voice she recognised as Xavier's. Guy's brother sounded furious. He was talking so rapidly that Amber didn't have a hope of translating it, but she could guess what he was saying—something along the lines of 'what the hell's going on?' She desperately wanted to pick up the phone and explain, but it wasn't her place—and, anyway, how could she explain?

Hell, hell, hell.

She'd wrecked Guy's life—and now she had to fix it.

Grim-faced, Amber picked up the phone. This was definitely a time when she needed help from her mother—and, even though she knew it would be a ridiculous time in LA, Libby would forgive her. Because this was important.

* * *

Guy was bone-deep tired by the end of the business day, and he knew it wasn't going to end here. He still had to get through the paparazzi, who were staked outside the perfume house and would no doubt be outside his flat, too. Amber had probably been trapped there all day. And he had to face her, too.

This was just like Véra all over again. If he hadn't let his heart overrule his head and got involved with her, this would never have happened.

How could he have been so stupid?

By the time he closed his front door, having ignored the cameras thrust in his face and the babbled questions of the journalists, he was in serious need of coffee and a sugar fix. He'd hated all the fuss when he'd split up with Véra, and he hated this even more. Because this time it wasn't just his personal life: it was his business. Everything he'd worked so hard to build.

'Guy?' Amber was sitting on the sofa, looking wary.

'I hate being doorstepped.' He raked a hand through his hair.

'I'm sorry.' She dragged in a breath. 'I know this whole thing has hurt you badly, hurt people you're close to, and I swear I never meant this to happen.'

He knew that. Of course she hadn't intended it. But it had still happened. And his life was sliding into the abyss.

'Guy, I… Look, I had a word with Mum's publicist this afternoon. We can fix this.'

'We?' He narrowed his eyes at her.

'I'm the reason you're in this mess in the first place. I got you in it, so I'm going to help get you out of it.'

He shook his head. 'I know you weren't the leak. It was your friend.'

'No. I already told you, she'd never do that. She's as

upset as I am, and she's found out what happened. She rang me back this afternoon.' She dragged in a breath. 'When Hugh went for that drink with his colleague, another colleague was there as well, with his girlfriend. Hugh accidentally mentioned my name and she put two and two together—I didn't see it, but apparently there were rumours in *Celebrity Life* last week that we were dating.'

'So this girlfriend told the press about me?' Guy really didn't get it. 'But I don't even know her. Why would she do that?'

Amber squirmed. 'I dated her boyfriend a couple of times—a year before he started seeing her, I might add, and it was over after the second date—and apparently she's a bit jealous. For some stupid reason, she got it into her head that I might be trying to get him back, so she decided to leak stuff to the press to make life hard for me and keep me away from her man. He's dumped her because of it, but…oh, it's just a mess.' She sighed. 'Bottom line, it's my fault—if I hadn't interfered and asked Hugh for advice, this wouldn't have happened. At least, not right now.'

Guy frowned. 'How do you mean, not right now?'

She bit her lip. 'I know you're angry with me, and I don't blame you. But, Guy, you couldn't keep a secret like that for ever. It was always going to come out.'

'Maybe. But not until after I'd fixed it.'

She took a deep breath. 'I know you don't want to hear this, but you need to face up to it. You've been searching for months and you haven't found a doctor who can help you. You might not be able to fix this, Guy. How long were you planning to follow the doctor's advice to wait and see?'

His face was expressionless. 'As long as it takes.'

'Which is what? A year? Five years? Guy, you said yourself that a perfume lasts for only two years. Which means you have, I don't know, maybe a year before you need to start developing the next one to replace the one you're about to launch. And if your sense of smell hasn't come back by then, you're going to need a contingency plan.'

'Become a business guru now, have you?' he asked, an edge to his voice.

She flinched. 'No. It's common sense. And, in the meantime, you can't just ignore the media.'

'Can't I? You're the one who says you can smile your way through everything.'

'Not with this, you can't. You have to talk to them, or they'll speculate and come up with even wilder theories.'

'And?'

'Just talk to the press, Guy. Tell them what you told me, about how you develop perfumes.'

He felt his lip curl. 'So they can dig around even more?'

'No, so they can see it from another side. If they see you as the underdog fighting hard to beat this thing, they'll be right behind you and they'll back you. Mum's publicist said she'd email me some ideas, but you need to work with them, Guy…'

'You forget,' he said, 'I've been here before. They dig and dig and dig and they never give up.'

'So the way round it is to give the press a story instead of making them work for it. Give them things they can work with. Make it easy for them, and they'll concentrate on the story you want them to tell. Make it hard, and they'll go for the jugular.'

'Right now,' Guy said, 'I'm too tired to think straight, let alone do anything.'

'Sit down. Let me make you some coffee, something to eat.'

'I'm not hungry.'

'Then can I run you a bubble bath or something?'

He shook his head. 'Amber, my career's going down the drain and you think a bubble bath is going to make everything all right?'

'No, but what do you expect me to do? Just walk out and leave you to it?' And then a nasty thought struck her. 'Is that what you want me to do? Go?'

'Right now, I don't know what I want,' he said.

Which made it pretty clear that he didn't want her, otherwise he'd have no doubts.

'But I doubt you'd get a flight to London until tomorrow,' he continued, 'and there's no point in fighting your way through the paparazzi only to sit in the airport all night, so you might as well stay.'

'I'll sleep on the sofa,' she said, 'so I don't disturb you.'

'You're my guest. *I'll* sleep on the sofa,' he said.

'Guy, I don't want to throw you out of your bed.' She wanted to share it with him. Hold him, let him know that she was going to support him and together they'd get through this mess.

'I'll sleep on the sofa,' he repeated tonelessly.

It looked as if he was going to keep her at arm's length. And there wasn't a thing Amber could do about it. So much for thinking that he was going to tell her he loved her. Right now, he loathed her—and she could understand why. Because of her, his whole life was in disarray. He was going to lose everything he'd worked so hard for.

Amber slept badly, that night. She knew Guy did, too, because she could see the faint glow from his laptop screen through the gap in the doorframe. She longed to go out there, put her arms round him and tell him she was going to make everything all right—but it would be an empty promise, because she couldn't fix the biggest problem for him. And if she pushed him the way Véra had, made him feel that she was demanding attention, it would only drive more of a wedge between them.

She just had to hope that if she gave him space, time to think, then he might forgive her—and give her the chance to help him fix as much of the damage as she could.

Guy felt like hell, the next morning. He could see dark circles under Amber's eyes when she emerged from the bedroom, and guessed she felt the same; obviously she'd slept as little as he had, the previous night.

He wished he hadn't been so stubborn. He was too tall to sleep comfortably on his sofa, and his back ached. Not that he would've slept properly in bed—he'd been too angry and miserable and frustrated to sleep—but he would at least have been lying in comfort. And with her in his arms.

'How are you?' she asked, her voice sounding scratchy from lack of sleep.

There was no point in pretending. They'd gone beyond that. 'Not good.' He paused. 'You?'

'Not good, either,' she whispered. 'I'm so sorry, Guy.'

He shrugged. 'You can't change the past.'

'If there's anything I can do—anything at all—'

'No,' he said.

He could see her blinking back the tears at his rejection. It really hadn't been her fault. He'd thought about it all night; and, although he was still angry at her friends for their carelessness, he knew she'd had the best of intentions. And, until everything had exploded yesterday, he'd actually been happy with her. 'Look, I have to go to work. We'll talk tonight,' he said, and walked over to the front door.

'Guy.'

'What?' He stopped with his fingers wrapped round the door handle.

'If you have dark glasses, wear them.' She drew a finger along the dark circles under her own eyes, the gesture telling him exactly why he needed to hide his eyes. 'And smile. The worse you feel, the harder you have to smile.'

'That sounds like experience talking.'

She nodded, clearly not trusting herself to speak.

He rummaged in a drawer and found his sunglasses. 'Thank you,' he said.

'You're welcome.'

And she looked so miserable that he couldn't resist touching her cheek with the backs of his fingers. 'We'll talk tonight,' he said softly, and left.

The paparazzi were waiting for him outside. And he took Amber's advice, lifted his chin and smiled. Smiled until his face hurt, all the way to the perfume house. His phone was already ringing as he walked in, and he spent the morning fielding calls at the same time as answering emails, persuading financiers and soothing concerned clients. It was utterly relentless, and he was near to breaking point when Simone, his secretary, brought in a pile of messages.

'Just bin them,' he said. The only people he wanted to talk to had already spoken to him or he was waiting for emails. 'I'm not talking to the press.'

'You might want to call this one back, Guy.' She looked sympathetically at him as she handed him the note.

Professor Pascal Marchand in Paris. It wasn't a name he'd come across before.

'He's a doctor,' Simone added helpfully.

A doctor? Why would a doctor be calling him? Unless… Hope surged through him. Was this the answer he'd been trying so hard to find? 'OK. I'll call him now.'

Please, please, let this be good news, he begged silently. Let this be someone who could help him. Let the professor be there and not tied up with patients for the rest of the day.

To his relief, the doctor's secretary put him through straight away.

'I'm doing a trial on anosmia,' Professor Marchand told him. 'I read about your case in the papers. I might be able to help you, if you're interested in taking part.'

Interested?

He could've kissed the man.

'I'm definitely interested,' Guy said. 'Thank you.'

'Would you be able to come to Paris for a discussion and some tests?'

'Absolutely,' Guy said. 'Just tell me where and when.'

By the end of the call, they'd arranged a meeting for Monday afternoon; and it felt as if the clouds had suddenly parted and let some sunlight in. Maybe, just maybe, this was going to work out.

He took his phone off the hook for a moment while he checked his emails. There was one from Amber, obviously forwarded from someone—her mother's publicist, he supposed. Advice on dealing with the media.

Now he'd had time to think about it, he knew that Amber had a point. He did have to deal with the media. And, given that talking to the press wasn't his favourite thing, he knew it made sense to take advice from a specialist in the field. Someone who knew what they were doing and could stop him repeating the kind of mistakes he'd made in the past.

He skim-read the email, and discovered that the publicist was incredibly down-to-earth and focused; everything he read was perfectly sensible rather than just a piece of fluff. He reread it and worked through the points more slowly, jotting notes on a pad as he did so. Half an hour later, he had a plan of campaign sorted and a phone interview booked with *What's Hot!*

By the end of the afternoon, there were still a lot of rough edges and things to sort out, but damage limitation was well under way. He had a new source of finance so he could buy Philippe's share of the perfume house, he had an appointment with the professor and now he knew exactly where he was going.

Which left one area of his life to sort out.

Amber.

They really, really needed to have that talk.

CHAPTER TWELVE

AMBER was just finishing packing when Guy walked in.

'What are you doing?' he asked.

'Getting out of your hair,' she said. 'Though I wasn't going to just leave you a note and run away, before you start thinking that. I was going to say goodbye to you myself. And to tell you how sorry I am that you've ended up hurt because of me.'

'You're leaving?'

He looked shocked. Not relieved. So did that mean he wanted her to stay? Dared she hope? 'Isn't that what you want?' she asked carefully.

'I…' He shrugged and spread his hands. 'Yes. And no.'

'That's not helpful, Guy.'

'I know,' he said. 'My head is saying yes, leave—because once you're out of the equation the press will see I'm just another boring businessman and ignore me. Just like they did when Véra and I finally split up.'

His head was telling him to make her leave. But he'd said yes *and* no. Which gave her some hope. 'So which bit of you is saying no?' she asked.

'Part of me that I can't trust. It led me wrong, the last time I followed it,' he said.

She frowned. 'I'm not with you.'

'My heart,' he explained. 'You and me, it's all been a rush. Just like it was with Véra.'

'I'm not Véra.'

'I know that,' he said softly, 'but there are an awful lot of parallels.'

'Like how?'

'I met her when she worked on the campaign for my last perfume for my old company. We had lunch together; she was charming, witty and incredibly beautiful, and I fell for her straight away. You know how you see someone for the first time and this zing goes straight through you?'

Just as it had when she'd first met him. She knew exactly what he was talking about.

'I asked her to have dinner with me that night.' He blew out a breath. 'It's not tactful, telling you this, and I apologise for that, but I need to be honest. It was intense as hell. We ended up in bed that night and stayed there all weekend.'

Again, very close to what had happened between them. Had it not been for the wedding breakfast, there was a very good chance that she and Guy wouldn't have got out of bed that morning. Or for the rest of the day, except to shower and maybe grab something from the kitchen.

'I asked her to marry me a week later. She said yes, and I thought she felt the same way about me as I did about her. We decided not to wait to get married—we did it as soon as we could sort out the paperwork, even though we'd barely known each other a month. Xav warned me not to rush into it and to give our relationship more time, but I didn't listen.' He shrugged. 'I was head over heels in love with her, and I thought it would be enough.'

He'd already told Amber about his divorce. 'But it wasn't,' she said softly.

'No. I nearly lost the perfume house over it, and I vowed

then I'd never allow myself to fall for anyone like her again. That I'd never let my heart rule my head.'

'So you're judging me on the same terms as your ex-wife? That's not fair. I'm not like her,' Amber said, more calmly than she felt. 'Yes, I'm from the same world, and I've made plenty of mistakes in my life, but I'm *not* like Véra.'

'I know. But, when I met you, there was that same immediate attraction.'

'So you think that means I'm going to be the same as her?' She shook her head in mingled sadness and annoyance. 'Then maybe it's just as well that I've packed.'

'You're not like her,' Guy said. 'And I don't want you to go.' He sighed. 'Hell, I'm making a mess of this. But right now, the way things are, I'm scared that I'm making the wrong choice, the way I did last time. You're from her world. I wasn't enough for her—and that was when I was starting up the perfume house and had the whole world at my feet. Now everything's hanging in the balance and I can't guarantee what's going to happen in the future, even though I think I'm on the way to fixing things.'

'What?' She stared at him in disbelief. 'You think it's all about money or status? Are you crazy? First of all, let me just remind you that I pay my own way. I'm not looking for a man to support me financially. God, the last thing I'd want is to have to account to a man for every single penny I spend on shoes, or my phone bill. It's up to me how I spend my money, and that's the way I like it.' She grimaced. 'This is the twenty-first century, not the nineteenth.'

Dull colour flooded his face. 'I didn't mean—'

Amber interrupted him. 'Do you want to know what I'm looking for? Before I came to France, I didn't know. But I do now. Being with you has shown me exactly what I want.' She lifted her chin. 'I want an equal partnership.

With someone I like being with, and who likes being with me. With someone who wants to be with me, but not every single second of the day. I want to do girly things with my friends, and I want my man to do his own things, too. It's our differences that'll make us interesting.' And then she stopped. 'My mouth's running away with me again. You haven't actually asked me for a relationship. And you've as good as said that I'm not what you're looking for.'

'We're from different worlds,' Guy said. 'You enjoy the spotlight.'

'Not all of it,' she said. 'But I like having fun and throwing parties and seeing my friends.'

'That's not me. I'm a nerdy scientist who leads a very quiet life.'

'Never the twain shall meet, hmm?' she said. 'This thing between us—it was only ever meant to be temporary. Hot sex.'

'And getting it out of our systems.' He looked at her. 'Is it out of yours, yet?'

'I don't know if I'm brave enough to answer that.' She bit her lip. 'How about you answer it first?'

'You're not out of my system, not by a long way. I like having you around. You've made me smile at a time of my life when it felt as if the world was about to end. You've made me see that, even if I never find a doctor to help me, my life's still got a lot going for it. I admit, my heart's panicking that you're a lot like Véra—but my head knows you're not.'

'And you trust your head.'

He nodded. 'You understand my work and I think you understand what makes me tick. But things aren't going to be easy. If my sense of smell comes back, I'm going to be working long hours at the parfumerie to keep my business plan on track,' he warned. 'And if it doesn't, I'm going to be hell to live with until I come to terms with it completely—and that might take me a while.'

'In any relationship, you take the rough with the smooth.' Amber paused. 'You said you didn't want a relationship.'

'So did you.' He met her gaze. 'What do you want?'

Crunch time.

'That's a hard one to answer,' she said.

'Why?'

'Because if I tell you that I want a proper relationship with you, that I want you to date me and for the world to know that you're my man, you'll think I'm needy like Véra, and it'll make you back off. And if I tell you that I'm fine with a temporary fling and hot sex, you'll think I'm shallow and I'll get bored, like your ex. Either way, I lose.' She sighed. 'What do I want? I want a man who's going to accept me—*love* me—as I am. Who's not going to try to pigeonhole me or control me or change me. Who can accept that I like parties and that I also like pottering around at home.'

'That you're the media darling and an angel of domesticity?'

'I'm no angel,' she said drily. 'I'm just me. Yes, I'm a fluffy socialite, and an airhead party girl. But you're the one who showed me I have depth.'

He nodded. 'And you're not an airhead. I guess it's possible to be more than one thing at the same time.'

'It is.' She paused. 'So let me ask you the same thing. What do you want?'

'You're right, that's hard to answer,' he said slowly. 'I want someone who understands me. Someone who understands that sometimes I'm going to be distracted and living in my head, when I'm creating a perfume, and who won't complain and expect me to drop everything for her. Someone who isn't going to mind that I don't want to live in Paris or New York or Rome—someone who's happy to split her time between the château and the perfume house, as I do.'

So what was he saying? That they didn't have a future? That he wouldn't compromise at all?

'But I also want someone,' he said softly, 'who knows how to have fun. Who'll stop me being too nerdy and serious. Someone who's impulsive and crazy enough to pose like one of my favourite paintings for me. Someone who has a different pair of high heels for every day of—well, at least a month, but I'd guess more like a year. Someone who believes that you can smile your way through almost anything and come out on top.'

Hope rushed through her. Everything he'd just said— that was her. And the way he'd put it, he wasn't going to try to change her or control her or pigeonhole her. 'So you'd take a chance on someone who has a bad track record when it comes to relationships?'

'If she'd do the same for me.' He paused. 'And I'm rather hoping that she's planning to cancel her flight, unpack her suitcase and put her stuff back in my wardrobe.'

'You're sure that's what you want?' There was one thing she knew was a huge issue between them. Something he'd find hard to accept. 'You can cope with the media hanging around us for a bit?'

'Being with you means being in the public eye, at least for some of the time.' He shrugged. 'I'll get used to it. But what I need—really need, right now—is you back in my arms.'

She smiled. 'I thought you'd never ask.'

Half a second later, his arms were wrapped round her and his mouth was jammed over hers. And he was kissing her as if his whole life depended on it.

'I'm sorry I've given you such a hard time,' he said, when he finally broke the kiss.

'It's OK. I understand why,' she said. 'In your shoes, I would've probably done the same.'

'That's more than I deserve.'

She laughed. 'I have ideas about how you can make it up to me.'

'And I'll look forward to hearing them,' he said. 'But there are some things I need to say to you, first.' He stroked her face. 'I love you, Amber—I really, *really* love you. You make my world a brighter place.'

'I love you, too.' She stroked his face. 'I think I fell for you the night of your brother's wedding, when you danced with me. Nobody had ever made me feel that hot and bothered before. I told myself it was just sex, but it wasn't.'

'No. It's a hell of a lot more. But, since you mentioned the *s*-word…'

A long, satisfying time later, Amber lay curled in Guy's arms.

'Something else I meant to tell you,' Guy said. 'Before you distracted me. I had a phone call today.'

She winced. 'Press?'

'A doctor. In Paris. He's running a trial on treating anosmia. I have an appointment with him on Monday afternoon, to see if I'm suitable for the trial.'

'That's brilliant news.' Amber brightened. 'I mean, I know there are no guarantees, but he's the first one who's said anything positive. That's a start.'

'A very good start,' he said.

'I, um, could go with you, if you like,' she offered. 'You know, for moral support and that.' She bit her lip. 'Actually, I'd probably better not. The press might hassle us.'

'They're already hassling me,' Guy pointed out. 'It's not going to make any difference whether they follow us to Paris or not. And yes, I'd like you to come with me. I could do with the moral support. Just in case—'

She pressed her finger to his lips to stop him. 'Don't borrow trouble. Wait and see what he says.' She raised an eyebrow. 'Clearly I'm going to have to distract you all weekend…'

Professor Marchand turned out to be in his late fifties, distinguished-looking and with a ready smile. He was relaxed about Amber staying with Guy for moral support, and she held Guy's hand through all the questions and the uncomfortable-looking procedure of having a tube up his nose with a camera. She had to stay in the waiting area while Guy had a CT scan, but then it was time to go back and see the professor for the verdict.

Guy's stomach was roiling and it was as much as he could do to put one foot in front of the other and rap on the doctor's open door.

But Professor Marchand was smiling as he looked up from the desk. 'Sit down,' he said.

Guy sat in silence, and felt the pressure of Amber's fingers against his.

'I'm afraid you're not going to be suitable for my trial,' he said.

Guy couldn't breathe, and he had no idea what the doctor said next. He'd hoped so much that the new treatment would be the answer. But now it seemed that he was going to have to live with it.

'Guy. *Guy.*' Amber nudged him. 'Did you hear what the professor said?'

'I'm looking for people with true anosmia,' Professor Marchand said, switching to English. 'And yours is fixable.'

Guy looked at him, shocked beyond belief. 'It is?'

'It's caused by a polyp in your sinus—so the tissue at the top of your nose, the one that affects your ability to smell, is fine. I think what happened is that the virus gave you sinusitis and a polyp developed. Your sense of smell got gradually worse since the virus, yes?'

Guy nodded. 'It's practically non-existent now.'

'Polyps are easy to fix.'

Guy couldn't take it in. 'But the last two specialists I saw—they couldn't find a thing.'

'You saw them, what, a month ago, two months?' Professor Marchand said. 'Maybe they were so small that they missed them. Or maybe, because your work is so sensitive, you reacted more strongly than the average person's nose would, out of proportion to the size of the polyps, so they thought there was another cause of the problem instead of seeing the obvious.'

It was fixable. Guy's heart was hammering so hard, he couldn't speak.

'The even better news,' Professor Marchand continued, 'is that the first-line treatment is a simple steroid spray to shrink the polyp. If this doesn't work, there are other treatments we can try, but the most important thing is that your sense of smell will definitely come back—even though I should warn you that it might take a while until it's back completely.'

Guy felt the blood thudding through his veins.

Everything was going to be all right.

'Thank God,' Amber breathed, still holding his hand tightly.

But he still had one burning question. 'Will the polyp come back?'

'If the medication doesn't work, or if the polyp comes back, we can try steroid tablets, or I can operate to remove it. The main thing is, it's fixable. You can stop worrying.

It's a shame for me that you're not suitable for my trial, because a man in your line of work would be an interesting case study—but I'm glad for you that you're not.'

'Thank you.' Guy shook the older man's hand, relief flooding through him. 'I can't say what this means to me. It's…' He was too choked to say any more.

'I'm glad I could help,' Professor Marchand said with a smile. He wrote a prescription. 'You need to take these daily—and you need to take them properly,' he said in English.

'Thank you.' Guy took the prescription.

'Call me if you're worried about anything.'

Guy smiled. 'I will.'

After they'd picked up the prescription and were back at the hotel, he enveloped Amber in a hug. 'It's going to be all right.' He blinked back the tears. 'I feel as if someone's taken the whole universe off my shoulders. And it's all because of you. If the story hadn't blown up in the media, Professor Marchand wouldn't have contacted me. And I would still be thinking that it wasn't fixable. My life would still be a mess.'

'I'm so glad it's worked out. That you're not going to have to live a nightmare any more.'

'No. I'm going back to living the dream. And I want to live it with you, Amber.' He paused, his eyes dark with sincerity. 'As my wife.'

No. He couldn't mean that. And what he'd just said: without her, he'd still be in a mess. He wasn't asking her because he couldn't live without her. 'You don't have to feel obliged to me. Or grateful. That's completely the wrong reason to propose to someone.'

'It's not the reason. I mean, of course I'm grateful to you—but I want to marry you because I want to be with you, Amber. You bring another dimension to everything.

Without you, nothing feels right. The whole heart of my world's missing. It's like a perfume with only a top and bottom note, nothing in between, and everything feels out of balance.'

He really felt like that about her?

Then again, that was the way he'd felt about Véra, and that had ended up badly, too.

'No,' she said. 'I'm still not going to marry you.'

He frowned. 'Why not? I love you, and you said that you loved me.'

'I do.'

'So what's the problem?'

'You married Véra in a rush and you regretted it. I don't want that to happen to us.'

'It won't happen to us.' He drew her hand up to his mouth and kissed it. 'And I know that because you're not like her and I was stupid ever to have thought you were. You come from the same world, yes, but you see things in a different way. We're both going to have to compromise to make this work, but I think we could do it.'

Compromise. That was the word she'd been looking for. 'All right, then, we'll compromise. If you're still sure in six months' time, ask me again and I'll say yes. But not until then.'

He frowned. 'So you don't believe we can make it?'

'Actually, I do,' she said, 'but I need to prove to both of us that it's not going to be like your last marriage. We're not going to rush into it, this time. We'll use our heads as well as our hearts. Besides, I still have things to do in England. I have a Christmas ball organised, and there will be things I need to sort out the week before—things I can't expect other people to pick up for me, because I'm the one who has all the notes and contact details.'

'Of course,' he said. 'I'm not expecting you to give up everything for me.'

'So what are you expecting?' she asked.

'To share my life with you,' he said simply. 'I have my work, you have your fundraising and your friends. But we'll have dinner together and ask each other about our day. Sometimes we'll go to parties. Sometimes we'll have quiet nights in at home.' He paused. 'And sometimes we'll be on the beach, making sandcastles with our children.'

She stared at him, not quite believing what she'd heard. 'You want children?'

'A family,' he said. 'With you, when we're both ready.'

He wanted to make a family with her. A family where she'd be loved for who she was. She had to blink back the tears. 'Oh, Guy. Six months,' she said, 'and then I want a *really* romantic proposal.'

He laughed. 'That's a deal.' And he kissed her, to prove it.

EPILOGUE

Six months later

'Guy, it's not even light yet,' Amber said, snuggling under the duvet. 'Go back to sleep for a little while.'

'Some of us have been up for half an hour already,' Guy said.

She opened her eyes and frowned. 'Why? Is something wrong?'

'No, but you need to get up, have a quick shower and get dressed. Don't ask questions, just trust me,' he added swiftly.

Amber gave up. 'OK, OK. Are you going to be fussy about what I wear, too?'

He indicated the dress hanging up on the door. 'That one.'

It was a shift dress in deep scarlet; Amber could see by looking at it that it was silk. And she'd never seen it before. And then she noticed that he was wearing a formal suit—something he never did for work. 'Guy?'

'No questions,' he reminded her. 'Oh, and no scent.'

'No scent?' She didn't have a clue why, but she'd learned over the last six months that when Guy was enthusiastic about something, it saved a lot of time to go along with him.

She showered, cleaned her teeth, brushed her hair and applied the bare minimum of make-up—just mascara and a slick of rose-coloured lipstick—then tried on the dress. It fitted perfectly; and Guy had left her the most gorgeous pair of shoes in the same colour, in the softest leather.

Wondering quite what he was planning, she headed downstairs. Guy came out of the kitchen, and smiled. 'Perfect. Come into the drawing room.'

She did as he said.

'Stay here—for, oh, two minutes, at most—and no peeping.'

'You're starting to get really annoying, do you know that?'

He simply laughed. 'In three minutes, you'll forgive me, *mon ange*.'

She wasn't so sure, but she stayed put until he came to fetch her. He led her through the French doors in the library through to the gardens at the back of the house, and then to the rose garden. She blinked in surprise as she saw a wrought-iron table set for two; it was lit with a dozen tiny tealight candles. There was a posy of roses in the middle—freshly cut from the garden, and still studded with silvery dew—next to a silver wine-cooler containing a bottle of champagne. And there was a basket of French pastries, still warm from the bakery.

Guy held her chair for her, then sat opposite. 'Now. Breakfast. A little later than the crack of dawn. Any second now...'

And the sun began to rise, casting a pinkish light over the roses.

'Good morning, *mon ange*,' he said with a smile.

She couldn't help smiling back. 'Guy, this is lovely.'

'So you forgive me for making you wake up so early,

now you know I wanted to have breakfast with you at sunrise?'

'Yes. Though I still don't understand why you wanted me to dress up.' She frowned. 'Or why you're wearing a suit.'

'That's the next bit.' He handed her a box, beautifully wrapped in white tissue paper with a gold chiffon ribbon. 'For you, *mon ange*.'

'For me? But, Guy, it's not my birthday for another two months.'

He rolled his eyes. 'I know. Just open it and put me out of my misery, will you?'

The box was way too big to contain a ring. Besides, he hadn't actually asked her to marry him…and that made her realise just how much she did want him to ask her. They'd agreed to give it six months, to see how things went, and every day she spent with Guy—whether it was in England, at Grasse or at the château—had made her happier and happier. She'd become involved in the perfume house, working on the new 'design your own scent' line and dealing with queries from the women's and lifestyle magazines, and she loved every second of her work. And Guy came with her to the glitzy parties, although she barely accepted half of the invitations nowadays, enjoying quiet nights in with her man as well.

It had worked out better than either of them had dreamed.

She undid the wrappings of the parcel, to reveal a plain white box with the GL Parfums logo.

And when she removed the lid, inside was a perfume flask—hand-blown amethyst-coloured glass, in the shape of a heart. 'Guy, this is beautiful.'

'That's the back, *mon ange*. Take a look at the other side.'

She turned the bottle over and there was an outline of a heart inscribed in amber-coloured gold on the glass. Inside, in a flowing script, were the words 'Amber of my heart.'

Her heart skipped a beat. 'What's this, a sneak preview of your new perfume?' The one she knew he'd been working on since the wildly successful launch of Angelique, and he'd gone all secretive and refused to let even her in his lab.

And he'd named it after her?

'It's what it says on the bottle.' He smiled at her. 'And no, this isn't for production. I had the flask designed by a new local craftsman, and it's exclusive. The perfume's a one-off, too. Like you.'

She couldn't quite take it in. 'You designed this for me.'

'Every bit of it is how I feel about you,' Guy said. 'I never told you this, *mon ange*, but I used to be able to see people in terms of scent. I lost that ability for a while, but you were instrumental in bringing it back to me. And this, to me, is you.'

'I…' She blinked back the tears. 'I don't know what to say.'

'Try it,' he invited. 'Tell me what you think it is.'

Now she knew why he'd told her not to wear scent. When she removed the glass stopper—coloured the same gold as the heart—there was an atomiser. She sprayed a little on her left wrist, and sniffed. 'This is lovely. An amber top note, right?'

'Absolutely. Give it ten minutes and you'll start to smell the roses—the very roses I was picking the same day I met you.' He indicated the roses around them. 'Which is why I wanted to give this to you, here. They're for your sweetness.'

She caught her breath.

'And your sensuality.' He grinned. 'I'm thinking of a certain Rossetti picture.'

She blushed, remembering the day she'd posed semi-naked for him in his lab with an armful of roses.

'And there's a base of tonka bean and vanilla; it reminds me of chocolate, the depth in the colour of your eyes and the silkiness of your hair. There are other layers in there, too, because you're complex—vetiver for sexiness and strength, citron for luminosity and cranberries because you're bright and sharp.' He ended his litany with a kiss. 'And I love you very, very much.'

It was a love letter in scent, and it rendered her temporarily speechless.

When she'd recovered herself enough to speak, she said, 'I love you, too, Guy. *Je t'aime. Toujours.*' She stroked the bottle. 'I can't believe you've called this by an English name, not French.'

'Because you're English—and anyway, as I told you, this isn't for production. This is exclusive. It's yours. Just like I am.' His eyes were utterly sincere. 'Always.'

'Guy, that's the nicest thing anyone's ever done for me,' she whispered.

He kissed away the single tear that slid down her cheek. 'Don't cry, *mon ange*. Not now. Because today's going to be a very special day. I hope.' Still holding her hand, he dropped down to one knee. He took a box from his pocket with his other hand, and opened it to reveal a perfect solitaire diamond. 'Amber Wynne—Amber of my heart—will you make me the happiest man in the world and do me the honour of becoming my wife?'

She cupped his face and lowered her mouth to kiss him lightly. 'Yes—oh, yes, *please*.'

He kissed her finger, then slid the ring onto it. It was a perfect fit, just as she knew it would be. Just as she and Guy were—and would be, for the rest of their days.

Coming Next Month

from **Harlequin Presents**®. Available January 25, 2011.

#2969 GISELLE'S CHOICE
Penny Jordan
The Parenti Dynasty

#2970 BELLA AND THE MERCILESS SHEIKH
Sarah Morgan
The Balfour Brides

#2971 HIS FORBIDDEN PASSION
Anne Mather

#2972 HIS MAJESTY'S CHILD
Sharon Kendrick

#2973 Gray Quinn's Baby
Susan Stephens
Men Without Mercy

#2974 HIRED BY HER HUSBAND
Anne McAllister

Coming Next Month

from **Harlequin Presents**® EXTRA. Available February 8, 2011.

#137 PROTECTED BY THE PRINCE
Annie West
The Weight of the Crown

#138 THE DISGRACED PRINCESS
Robyn Donald
The Weight of the Crown

#139 WHEN HE WAS BAD...
Anne Oliver
Maverick Millionaires

#140 REBEL WITH A CAUSE
Natalie Anderson
Maverick Millionaires

HPECNM0111

REQUEST YOUR FREE BOOKS!

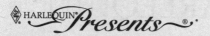

2 FREE NOVELS PLUS
2 FREE GIFTS!

YES! Please send me 2 FREE Harlequin Presents® novels and my 2 FREE gifts (gifts are worth about $10). After receiving them, if I don't wish to receive any more books, I can return the shipping statement marked "cancel." If I don't cancel, I will receive 6 brand-new novels every month and be billed just $4.05 per book in the U.S. or $4.74 per book in Canada. That's a saving of at least 15% off the cover price! It's quite a bargain! Shipping and handling is just 50¢ per book.* I understand that accepting the 2 free books and gifts places me under no obligation to buy anything. I can always return a shipment and cancel at any time. Even if I never buy another book, the two free books and gifts are mine to keep forever.

106/306 HDN E5M4

Name _____ (PLEASE PRINT) _____

Address _____ Apt. # _____

City _____ State/Prov. _____ Zip/Postal Code _____

Signature (if under 18, a parent or guardian must sign) _____

Mail to the **Harlequin Reader Service:**
IN U.S.A.: P.O. Box 1867, Buffalo, NY 14240-1867
IN CANADA: P.O. Box 609, Fort Erie, Ontario L2A 5X3

Not valid for current subscribers to Harlequin Presents books.

Are you a current subscriber to Harlequin Presents books and want to receive the larger-print edition? Call 1-800-873-8635 today!

* Terms and prices subject to change without notice. Prices do not include applicable taxes. N.Y. residents add applicable sales tax. Canadian residents will be charged applicable provincial taxes and GST. Offer not valid in Quebec. This offer is limited to one order per household. All orders subject to approval. Credit or debit balances in a customer's account(s) may be offset by any other outstanding balance owed by or to the customer. Please allow 4 to 6 weeks for delivery. Offer available while quantities last.

Your Privacy: Harlequin Books is committed to protecting your privacy. Our Privacy Policy is available online at www.eHarlequin.com or upon request from the Reader Service. From time to time we make our lists of customers available to reputable third parties who may have a product or service of interest to you. If you would prefer we not share your name and address, please check here. ☐

Help us get it right—We strive for accurate, respectful and relevant communications. To clarify or modify your communication preferences, visit us at www.ReaderService.com/consumerschoice.

HP10R

HARLEQUIN®

A Romance

FOR EVERY MOOD™

Spotlight on
Classic

Quintessential, modern love stories
that are romance at its finest.

See the next page
to enjoy a sneak peek from
the Harlequin® Romance series.

Harlequin Romance author Donna Alward is loved for her gorgeous rancher heroes.

Meet Wyatt as he's confronted by both a precious little pink bundle left on his doorstep and his neighbor Elli who's going to show him the ropes....

Introducing
PROUD RANCHER, PRECIOUS BUNDLE

THE SQUAWKING QUIETED as Elli picked the baby up, and Wyatt turned around, trying hard to ignore the feelings of inadequacy as Darcy immediately stopped fussing.

"Maybe she's uncomfortable. What do you think, sweetheart?" Elli turned her conversation to the baby.

"What do you think is wrong?" Wyatt asked, putting the coffee pot back on the burner.

A strange look passed over Elli's face, one that looked like guilt and panic. But it was gone quickly. "I couldn't say," she replied.

"But you were so good with her this afternoon." Wyatt put his hands on his hips.

"Lucky, that's all. I just...remembered a few things." The same strange look flitted over her features once more.

Wyatt took the coffee to the table. "You fooled me. You looked like you knew exactly what you were doing." So much so that Wyatt had felt completely inept. A feeling he despised. He was used to being the one in control.

Elli and Darcy walked the length of the kitchen and back. After a few moments, she admitted, "I haven't really cared for a baby before. The things I thought of were simply things I'd heard about. Not from experience, Mr. Black."

Her chin jutted up, closing the subject but making him

want to ask the questions now pulsing through his mind. But then he remembered the old saying—*Don't look a gift horse in the mouth*. He'd benefit from whatever insight she had and be glad of it.

"I don't really know what babies need," he said. "I fed her, patted her back like you did, walked her to sleep, but every time I put her down…"

Wyatt almost groaned. Of course. He'd forgotten one important thing. He'd been so focused on getting the formula the right temperature that he'd forgotten to check her diaper. Not that he had any clue what to do there either.

Pulling calves and shoveling out stalls was far less intimidating than one tiny newborn.

"She's probably due for a diaper change, isn't she." He tried to sound nonchalant. This was a perfect opportunity. Elli must know how to change a diaper. He could simply watch her so he'd know better for the next time.

Instead, Elli came around the corner of the counter and placed Darcy back in his arms. "Here you go, Uncle Wyatt," she said lightly. "You get diaper duty. I'll fix the coffee. Cream and sugar?"

Oh boy, Wyatt thought, looking down into Darcy's pursed face, his smug plan blown to smithereens. He was in for it now.

Will sparks fly between Elli and Wyatt?

Find out in
PROUD RANCHER, PRECIOUS BUNDLE
Available February 2011 from Harlequin Romance

Try these Healthy and Delicious Spring Rolls!

INGREDIENTS

2 packages rice-paper
spring roll wrappers
(20 wrappers)

1 cup grated carrot

¼ cup bean sprouts

1 cucumber, julienned

1 red bell pepper, without
stem and seeds, julienned

4 green onions
finely chopped—
use only the green part

DIRECTIONS

1. Soak one rice-paper wrapper
   in a large bowl of hot water
   until softened.

2. Place a pinch each of carrots,
   sprouts, cucumber, bell
   pepper and green onion on the
   wrapper toward the bottom
   third of the rice paper.

3. Fold ends in and roll tightly
   to enclose filling.

4. Repeat with remaining
   wrappers. Chill before
   serving.

Find this and many more delectable recipes
including the perfect dipping sauce in

YOUR BEST BODY NOW
by
TOSCA RENO

WITH STACY BAKER

Bestselling Author of
THE EAT-CLEAN DIET®

Available wherever books are sold!

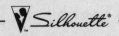

SPECIAL EDITION

FROM *USA TODAY* BESTSELLING AUTHOR

CHRISTINE RIMMER

COMES AN ALL-NEW BRAVO FAMILY TIES STORY.

Donovan McRae has experienced
the greatest loss a man can face, and
while he can't forgive himself, life—
and Abilene Bravo's love—are still
waiting for him. Can he find it in himself
to reach out and claim them?

Look for

DONOVAN'S CHILD

available February 2011